AWKWARD RELATIONSHIPS SHORT STORY COLLECTION VOL. II

AWKWARD RELATIONSHIPS SHORT STORY COLLECTION VOL. II

VALENCIA N LEE

CONTENTS

To my moma, I know you in Heaven looking down on me

Her 13th Birthday

When Toya was 12 years old, her world was turned upside down when her dad unexpectedly showed up at her mom's house, accompanied by his new wife and six children. Toya and her mother were taken aback; it had been three long years since they had seen him. Toya was his only child, and the last news she had heard from her aunt was that he was in another state, on the run from the police.

Toya's mom was furious, her anger simmering beneath the surface. After all, she hadn't received child support in over five years. The last check had arrived at a measly $1.08. But she was skilled at masking her rage. To everyone else, she appeared composed. Toya, however, could read her mother like an open book.

That evening, they all sat outside on the front porch. Toya's mom made it clear that she wouldn't be letting any strangers into her house, especially her dad. She peppered her dad's new wife with questions, curious about how they had met and how long she had known him. Toya's new stepmom replied that they had met in Los Angeles, California. As the conversation unfolded, Toya stared up at the moon, feeling a strange longing—it seemed closer than ever, and for a moment, she imagined she could reach out and touch it.

Toya was stunned by her mom's unpredictable behavior. In one breath, her mother engaged in polite conversation with her father and his new wife, while Toya waited anxiously for her to unleash the torrent of emotions she must have felt inside. Considering her dad's past—a three-time felon with a rap sheet the size of a dictionary—Toya knew her mother could have said plenty about him. But surprisingly, she remained silent, allowing him to bask in the facade of normalcy.

Toya's new step-siblings were all older than her, ranging from 13 to 19 years old, with one of the boys already an adult. They appeared to be a close-knit group, laughing and joking together, while Toya felt more like an outsider. When her dad extended an invitation for her to spend the upcoming Christmas holidays with them, Toya's mother immediately shot it down.

"I'm not ready for you to go to another state for an extended visit without me," she asserted firmly. For the first time, Toya found herself agreeing with her mom.

The following year, things between Toya and her mother had become strained. They seemed to argue every day, their relationship unraveling under the weight of frustration and misunderstandings. In a moment of exasperation, her mom called Toya's dad and decided to send Toya to California for the summer, believing it would be better for both of them. She even bought her a plane ticket without consulting her.

Toya felt a mixture of anxiety and uncertainty about what to expect in a different state. She had never been away from her mom for more than two days, and those were spent at basketball camp where she cried every night from homesickness.

When she finally arrived at the airport in California, Toya stepped off the plane, scanning the crowd for her dad. But there was no sign of him. Her heart sank, thinking he was once again playing the role of the irresponsible and neglectful parent. With just $47 in her pocket and a rumbling stomach, she decided to stop at Pappasito's for a quick meal.

It was thirty minutes later when her oldest stepbrother, Xan, approached her. "Mind if I have some of your fajitas?" he asked, a serious look on his face. Though she was reluctant to share, she handed him a taco, wishing she didn't have to part with any of her food.

An hour later, they drove into a small country town, pulling up to a tiny wooden house situated on five acres of land. It was nothing like the glamorous Los Angeles Toya had seen on TV. The property was filled with cows, chickens, and goats, and Toya felt a strange mix of fascination and disappointment. Her gaze was drawn to a vibrant garden brimming with colorful fruits and vegetables. She wandered over to introduce herself to her stepmom, who was sipping wine in the garden. "You can call me Ms. Judy," her stepmom said, but Toya insisted on calling her "stepmom," wanting to establish a sense of closeness.

As she entered the house, Toya caught sight of her dad, lounging outside beside the garage with an unfamiliar guy, smoking a joint. Inside, the house felt cramped. There were only three rooms, and now Toya had to share a room with three other girls, all of whom had bunk beds. The boys shared another room next door, and they all had to share a single bathroom. Gone were the days of leisurely thirty-minute showers; now, Toya was restricted to five minutes—seven at most.

To make matters worse, there was a weekly chore list that everyone had to follow. Toya was responsible for washing dishes and doing her own laundry. What stung the most was the realization that she had to ask permission every time she wanted to eat something from the kitchen.

On top of that, she found herself milking cows, collecting eggs, and cleaning fish whenever her dad went fishing. Even the few candy bars she indulged in had to be shared with her siblings, which led her to start hiding her belongings. However, it didn't take long for them to discover her hiding spots.

As the days rolled on, Toya fell into a deep depression, feeling more and more homesick. The first week in California felt unbearable, and she longed to return to Houston, Texas, where she felt safe and loved.

Despite her pleas to her mom to let her come home, she was told she had to stay. "You're on vacation," her mother insisted, unaware of the turmoil Toya was experiencing.

Toya found herself sleeping throughout the day, only waking around dinner time. Her step-siblings, busy with their jobs or summer school, went to bed early, leaving Toya with the quiet house. In those solitary hours, she indulged in her favorite television shows, grateful for the access to Showtime and HBO that kept her entertained.

On weekends, her two oldest step-brothers would venture out to pick up their girlfriends from the gentleman's club between 3:00 and 4:00 AM. Xan's girlfriend, Susie, drove a sleek drop-top BMW with shiny, glistening 20-inch rims. She often let Xan borrow her car, which meant Toya could hitch a ride when he went to collect her.

When Susie worked late, they sometimes wandered into the club. It was the most fascinating scene Toya had ever encountered. She used to think that Six Flags was the best place in the world, but this club was something entirely different. The atmosphere was intoxicating, and the pulsating energy mesmerized her. Surrounded by dollar bills scattered across the floor and stage, with half-naked women captivating the crowd, Toya thought she had discovered paradise. She couldn't wait for her own chance to grow up and possibly work in a place like that one day.

Toya didn't spend a lot of time with her step-sisters; they didn't share the same interests or go out for fun like Xan did. However, she grew close to Susie over time. On Susie's days off, she would pick Toya up, drop the top on her BMW, and take her to the mall or for a leisurely day out.

Susie encouraged Toya to engage with guys, challenging her to see how many phone numbers she could collect. "Your Texas accent is attractive to California guys," Susie would say, taking Toya under her wing. With her help, they explored the local scene, meeting new people and having fun, a welcome distraction from the difficulties Toya had faced since moving.

For Toya's 13th birthday, her stepmom organized a spectacular celebration before they returned to Texas. The festivities included a lively parade featuring dance teams, and her stepmom enlisted the entire community to contribute dishes for a beach party. There were hamburgers, lamb chops, and an array of baked, fried, and grilled fish, providing enough food to last everyone the entire week.

Later that evening, Susie and some of her friends from the club came over to join Toya's sleepover. Eagerly, Toya turned to Susie and asked about her birthday present. Susie laughed, assuring her she would get her gift later.

Around 2:00 AM, Toya's stepmom excitedly announced that she had found the scariest movie she could think of: Halloween. With more than 30 guests settled in for the night at Toya's dad and stepmom's house, the atmosphere crackled with energy. Exhausted from the day's events, Toya took a shower, then grabbed her blanket and pillow before lying down on the floor between her stepsisters. Everyone else at the sleepover consisted of guys and friends of her stepbrothers, creating a lively and bustling environment around her.

Toya was asleep while the credits on the movie were still showing. It wasn't long before she was awakened by someone under her covers. It took her a while to open her eyes as she squirmed herself awake. Finally, she pulled up the blanket she was lying under, and she saw a faded haircut with deep waves and another head with an Afro. The guy with the afro looked up at Toya and put his pointer finger in front of his lips, telling her to be quiet. She wanted to scream as one of them pulled down her pants. Then Susie came and sat near her on the couch while the two guys licked her in different places. Susie told her to just chill and allow them to show her what it felt like to be a woman. Susie told her that since she was 13 years old, she was a woman now and she needed to start doing womanly things.

Every Time Her Husband Cheated On Her

Ciara and her husband, Sonny, relocated to Milwaukee, Wisconsin, after he accepted a position as President at a university. Sonny persuaded Ciara to migrate to the new town by gifting her a five-carat diamond ring and purchasing her dream house. Ciara also got a new Mercedes G wagon to go along with it. The icing on the cake was Sonny agreed to go to marriage counseling twice a week and he promised not to cheat on Ciara ever again. It had been exactly 8 months, and things between them were finally getting back to normal.

Sonny and Ciara had been married for 17 years. Although Sonny bought these material gifts and showed Ciara more love and affection, she knew she would never be enough for him. Sonny wanted a big family with five or more kids. Unfortunately, Ciara was unable to bear any children. They'd tried everything and spent over $500,000 but nothing seemed to work. Ciara tried to be the best wife she could be to Sonny anyways. She was a caring stepmother to Sonny's two illegitimate kids that he'd conceived during the last decade of their marriage. Then a few months passed by, Sonny started coming home late again or not at all. Ciara stayed home, cleaned, and made dinner for him every night, but he was never there to enjoy it. She was nearly 50 years old but she decided she didn't want to continue living like this.

One day Ciara unexpectedly went to the college to visit Sonny. Her presence shocked his assistant because she didn't know Sonny was married. She called Ciara, Shante, another woman's name. While Sonny's assistant was trying to figure out who she was. Ciara noticed Sonny

Mitchell listed on the door behind his assistant. So she marched past his gatekeeper and into his office. Sonny hurdled from the couch and ran as if he'd seen a ghost. He quickly pulled up his pants and tried to fix his neck tie. The young woman pulled down her skirt and wiped her mouth. It was evident what was going on. Ciara put her hand out and introduced herself to the young lady. Speechless, the lady shook her hand. Then Ciara invited her over to dinner that night and told Sonny he better be there also. Ciara went home and began preparing dinner for Sonny and his new mistress. Ciara sat at the dinner table alone with three medium-rare cooked steaks, stuffed baked potatoes, asparagus, a chef's salad, and two empty bottles of Moscato. She waited and waited. It was midnight, and no one showed.

A couple of days had gone by, and Ciara hadn't seen her husband. She went back to the campus and sat outside the administration building where Sonny worked. As she sat there, the young woman she caught Sonny with in his office passed by her. Ciara stopped her and reminded her who she was. The lady tried to run away, but Ciara grabbed her with a tight grip on her left arm. Finally, the young lady stopped struggling to get away and apologized. Ciara asked her what her name was and she responded, Reese. Reese explained that Sonny told her that his wife was dead and she felt sorry for him. Ciara forgave her because she was only maybe 19 or 20 years old. Ciara told her she could make it up to her by meeting her for dinner that night. Reese promised she would be in attendance this time.

Reese and Ciara met around 8:00 that night at Perry's Steakhouse. Ciara wore a black dress with a white stripe on the right side and a high split on the other. She wore white gold accessories and shoes to match her dress. Ciara ordered steaks, lobster, salmon, lamb chops, and a seafood platter. She filled Reese up with lots of champagne. Reese started vomiting information to Ciara. She shared with her that she was a senior at the university studying psychology, and she wanted to be a Licensed Practitioner Counselor. She only needed 24 more hours to graduate but she was unable to attend the previous semester because she didn't have tuition money. So she explained she met Sonny at the university one night while cleaning the building where the professors held their staff meetings. Afterwards, Sonny invited her out for a drink at the bar and they were intimate the same night and he has been paying her tuition and rent for her apartment ever since.

Ciara explained to Reese that was her money and not Sonny's. Her father owned multiple real estate and marketing companies and sold the companies ten years ago before he passed away and profited ten times more than the original net worth. Ciara was the only child, and her inheritance was enough for the next three generations. They stayed at Perry's Steakhouse until it closed. They were both intoxicated. Neither could drive so they shared an Lyft back to Reese's apartment. After arriving, Reese shared with Ciara the text messages Sonny sent her while they were at the restaurant. Sonny was furious Reese was ignoring him. They listened to Sonny's messages, laughed, and they both fell asleep.

The following morning, Ciara went home and Reese went to class. To Ciara's surprise, Sonny was at home getting ready for work. He had an attitude with her for being out all night. He was slamming doors, breaking dishes, and throwing trash all over the house. Ciara sat at the dinner table and thought about all the times Sonny cheated on her as he went on his rant. She texted Reese and told her how Sonny was acting and Reese agreed to let Ciara stay with her for a few days.

A week later, Ciara went back home. Sonny was sitting on the couch and dressed up in his black leather jacket. Ciara approached him and asked where he was going. Sonny told Ciara that his ex-girlfriend, Camille, was in town, and he was showing her around the city. Ciara went upstairs to change clothes. As Sonny was leaving, Ciara followed behind him as if she was going to. Sonny told her she wasn't invited. She asked him if he thought it was okay to go out with his high school sweetheart without her. Sonny laughed and continued walking out the back door, and got into her car. Sonny not knowing Ciara put a GPS tracker on his car. She followed him.

Thirty minutes later, Ciara met Sonny and Camille at Max's Chicken and Wine. They were sitting in the corner in a booth sipping a glass of wine. Sonny's arm was wrapped around Camille, and she was wiping his face with a napkin when Ciara approached them. She joined them and sat on the other side of the booth. She introduced herself to Camille as Sonny's wife. Camille was shocked because Sonny told Camille he was divorced from his wife. The waitress came to their table and asked if they were ready to order. Ciara answered yes and told the waitress her order. Sonny got upset. You could see the veins in his head bustling out. After twenty minutes of Sonny and Ciara arguing, the waitress brought their food to the table. Sonny was furious and decided to leave Ciara and Camille at the restaurant. Camille was hungry and chose to stay. She apologized to Ciara about Sonny and told her she'd been married seven times and respected marriages. Ciara and Camille stayed at the restaurant until they closed. Ciara expressed to Camille that she didn't want to go home that night. Camille invited Ciara to stay at her Air BNB for a couple of days.

Staying with Camille was so refreshing. Every night Camille held Ciara in her arms until she fell asleep and listened to all that Sonny had put Ciara through during their marriage. Ciara thought Camille was sweet, genuine, and nurturing. Too good for Sonny. The first time Camille and Ciara were intimate, Camille was patient with her. Ciara never experienced being naked in her skin like she did with Camille. She was myself. She didn't need any makeup, lipstick, or any other facial alterations. Ciara stayed with Camille for eight days. She hated Camille was going back to Washington, D.C., in a couple of days. She was going to miss her. But Camille promised her they would see each other again.

Ciara went back home. When she arrived, a gorgeous, young woman was vacuuming her house. She was confused because she did all the house chores. Ciara introduced herself to her. The lady told her that her name was Veronica. Ciara proceeded to ask questions, but before the lady could answer, Sonny interrupted their conversation. He introduced Veronica and her two kids to Ciara. Sonny said the lady was his childhood friend and Veronica had been dealing with domestic violence and needed somewhere to stay. Sonny kissed Veronica on her forehead and told her she could stay as long as she needed. Sonny picked up her youngest son and they excitedly ran outside with her eldest son following. Ciara went to the refrigerator and grabbed her bottle of Don Julio Reposado. Veronica and Ciara conversed for at least an hour while Sonny and her kids were outside. Ciara was comforting and understanding about her situation.

Later that night, Sonny fell asleep after dinner and Veronica made the boys go to sleep. Veronica and Ciara popped open a bottle of Crown Royal. Veronica laughed when she saw Ciara put Skittles in her drink. They talked all nigh and eventually fell asleep on the hammock outside till the sun came up. That morning, Veronica began crying and heavily pouring tears on Ciara's shoulder. Ciara comforted her and caressed her head until she calmed down. She assured Veronica that everything would be okay. Then Veronica looked deep down into Ciara's eyes and kissed her on the forehead, then again on her lips. Veronica asked Ciara if they could sleep like that every night.

It Costs to Keep the Coochie Clean

When Sarah was 11 years old and her younger sister, Deja, was 10, they would often spend the weekends at their Aunt Dee Dee's house. At 24 years old, Aunt Dee Dee was their mother's younger sister, but she felt more like an older sister to them.

Aunt Dee Dee lived a glamorous lifestyle that Sarah, Deja, and all their friends admired. She resided in a stylish two-story townhome that came with access to a community pool. The neighborhood clubhouse was a hub of activity, featuring pool tables, ping-pong tables, and several arcade games. Whenever they visited, Aunt Dee Dee would take Sarah and Deja to the clubhouse.

Sarah adored playing "Cruisin' the USA," her favorite arcade game, while Deja spent most of her time on the karaoke machine, belting out the hottest 90s hits. The weekends with Aunt Dee Dee were always filled with fun, laughter, and the thrill of new adventures.

Spending time with Aunt Dee Dee felt like a mini-vacation for Sarah and Deja, bringing them peace of mind. Aunt Dee Dee was well-connected in the neighborhood; everyone knew who she was and respected her. They also made it clear they cared for Sarah and Deja, ensuring they were treated well. Thanks to Aunt Dee Dee, they enjoyed free access to movies, bowling alleys, and skating rinks.

More importantly, Aunt Dee Dee acted as their therapist. She always took the time to ask how they were doing and wanted to know what was happening in their lives. Sometimes, Sarah found herself getting irritated by her aunt's probing questions, feeling she was just being nosy.

Yet, deep down, she appreciated Aunt Dee Dee's efforts to check in on her and Deja throughout the week, making sure they had essentials like toilet paper and food, and that the utilities were on. It was comforting to know that they had their Aunt Dee Dee.

Sarah and Deja's parents fell victim to the crack epidemic, leaving them in a state of uncertainty. They never knew when or if their parents would come home. As the eldest, Sarah took it upon herself to ensure Deja got to and from school safely and had clean clothes and enough food to eat.

Aunt Dee Dee lived just a few blocks away. Whenever she wasn't working overtime at the hospital or taking on her part-time job in home health care, she made it a point to drive Sarah and Deja to school. Dee Dee cherished those moments, enjoying the chance to be involved in her nieces' lives. However, Deja often dreaded these walks because Aunt Dee Dee would sometimes be in her nightgown, sporting a hair bonnet with rollers still in her hair. Sarah would burst into laughter at the sight, while Deja would walk far ahead of them, eager to distance herself from the embarrassment.

When Sarah and Deja spent the night at Aunt Dee Dee's house, they often found themselves awakening around 3:00 AM to one of the most awkward moments imaginable. After a fun-filled evening of swimming, watching movies, and playing video games, they would be completely exhausted. But Aunt Dee Dee would wake them up, wearing her nightgown, her infamous hair bonnet perched on her head, and a facial mask covering her face. At that moment, Sarah and Deja would feel as though they were in a dream.

Aunt Dee Dee would call out, "Yes, it's that time of the night, y'all—get up!" The girls knew exactly what she meant, but they would often close their eyes and hope she would forget.

To block her out, Sarah rolled over and pulled the blankets over their heads. But Aunt Dee Dee was relentless; she poked Sarah with a broom to wake her up. When they got up, she handed both girls colorful square packages. Some were wrapped in shiny gold paper. Deja, excited at first, thought it was candy. But when she tore one open, she was stunned to find a slimy, round, unappetizing item inside. Disgusted, she threw it on the floor, but Aunt Dee Dee immediately ordered her to pick it back up.

Aunt Dee Dee gave them the same leisure she gave them any time they spent the night at her house. She told them that every time they had sex, they needed to use a condom. Dee Dee pulled a condom out of the bag with one hand and ripped it open with her mouth. She put one finger inside and slowly began rolling it back. Then she took the condom, placed it on the broomstick between her legs, and rolled it back until it wouldn't anymore. She reminded them to make sure the condom fitted properly because there would be consequences if it didn't.

Aunt Dee Dee was Sarah and Deja's role model and the most incredible person in the world until she made them do this. She would wake them out of their sleep to put condoms on vacuum cleaners, cucumbers, pickles, bananas, or anything else shaped like a penis. She printed pictures of venereal diseases and made them view images of genital warts. Their parents didn't tell them about the birds and the bees, so Aunt Dee Dee made it her responsibility. One night, Aunt Dee Dee attempted to penetrate a pickle in a straw. She told them that their first time having sex would feel like that. Although they didn't understand her analogy, the pickle wouldn't fit through the straw. It looked excruciating.

By the time Sarah turned 16, she began liking boys. Although she had always been a tomboy and heavily into sports, she started dating. Meanwhile, Deja took a different path than Sarah and chose to save herself for marriage. But as Sarah watched all her friends engaging in relationships and discussing their sexual experiences, she couldn't help but feel curious about the excitement Aunt Dee Dee talked to them about. Wanting to learn more, she decided to confide in Aunt Dee Dee about her feelings.

Aunt Dee Dee sat Sarah and Deja down for a heart-to-heart conversation. She made it clear that one of the things many boys appreciate is when women take care of their appearance, and this extends to the choice of lingerie and undergarments. To emphasize her point, she took them on a trip to Victoria's Secret. As they entered the store, the displays of elegant bras and beautiful panties drew them in. Dee Dee guided them through the aisles, pointing out various styles that not only looked stunning but also made a statement about confidence and femininity. She picked up a few items and revealed the price tags, emphasizing the investment women often make to feel attractive and desirable for the opposite sex.

After their shopping excursion, they returned home with new insights and a few enticing purchases. Aunt Dee Dee then led them to the pantry, not to show off snacks, but to share a different kind of knowledge. She opened the cupboard and revealed her stash of feminine hygiene products: soaps, body washes, pads, tampons, panty liners, toilet paper, body sprays, and lotions. Each item served a purpose in maintaining personal care and hygiene, and she explained the importance of each one.

With a calculator in hand, Aunt Dee Dee began to tally up the monthly costs associated with these essential products. The numbers added up surprisingly quickly, giving them a clearer picture of what managing such expenses entails.

As she wrapped up the discussion, Aunt Dee Dee looked them in the eye and firmly but with a caring tone said, "Before you decide to get some penis, remember: It Costs to Keep the Coochie Clean!" Her statement was not just a playful reminder but a serious consideration of the responsibilities that come with being an adult. It was a lesson in self-care, empowerment, and the understanding that every choice has its associated costs, both financially and emotionally.

She Trapped Him

Melissa was 35 when she was released from the halfway house and moved back home with her moma. She'd served ten years in prison for drug possession and intent to distribute. She had thirteen-year-old twin boys, Mitch and Mike, who lived with her older brother, Joseph.

Joseph had custody of Mitch and Mike while Melissa was incarcerated. Joseph banned her from his home and Melissa was not allowed to see her sons. Melissa hadn't seen them in almost 11 years. While living with her moma, Melissa attempted to go to court to fight Joseph's decision, but the judge agreed with him. Melissa continued to reach out to Mike and Mitch multiple times, but she got no response. Her moma demanded she get a job. Melissa fell into manic depression and started stealing her mom's pain medication.

After a couple of weeks, Melissa had taken all of her mom's medication. She needed more so she decided to explore her old neighborhood in search of finding a familiar face whom she could get drugs from. While walking, she ran into an childhood friend named Daniel. She'd known him since elementary school. His grandparents lived two doors down from her mom's house. Daniel's grandparents passed away and left him the house. Daniel always had Melissa's back. He was a couple of years younger than her. He would steal candy and juice from the store for Melissa when they were younger. Daniel was like a younger brother to Melissa and she never saw a future with him until now.

When they were younger, Daniel and Melissa robbed a local grocery store. Daniel got caught and Melissa got away. They told Daniel they would let him go if he snitched on the other person with him, but he didn't tell on Melissa. He went to juvenile instead. Daniel went to jail plenty of times after that for theft and robbery. The state gave him the option to go into the military or prison when he was 18 years old. He chose the military.

As Melissa and Daniel stood outside talking, Daniel bragged about how the military changed his life. Recently, Daniel returned from the United States Marine Corps, and it was something about him that Melissa was attracted to now. He'd gained 20 pounds of muscle, was confident, and had gotten his crooked smile fixed. Melissa wanted Daniel in every way she could. She planned to pursue him like a roach pursued a crumb for dinner when the lights went out.

While conversing with Daniel, Melissa noticed that Daniel still saw the best in her. He complimented her often. In less than a week, Melissa and Daniel began dating. He took her to fancy restaurants so she could experience the different foods he tried while traveling. Sometimes Melissa couldn't read or pronounce the items on the menu. The waiter or waitress would stare at her. She would be embarrassed and could feel that they thought she was ignorant. Melissa tried to act intelligent while out with Daniel though and not show that she was a high school dropout, but the thought made her angry. She would curse them out and Daniel would jump in and defend her. Daniel, on the other hand, spoke six different languages and had traveled across the world. He'd earned a bachelor's degree in Business and planned to get his Master's in Business Administration. Most of the time when Daniel spoke to Melissa about traveling and living in different places, she didn't know what he was talking about or referring to. She just sat there and listened as if she was interested.

A year later, Daniel purchased a house near Lake Travis in Austin, Texas. It was an hour away from where they were originally from. He'd gotten the kitchen and bathroom remodeled. And added a hot tub in their bedroom. Daniel's house was twice as large as his grandparent's house, which they shared back home. Melissa enjoyed waking up every morning, looking down at the lake, and watching the sunrise while smoking a joint. Daniel disapproved of her smoking and expressed it was unladylike. Melissa stopped for one day. She started going for a run around the trial on Lake Travis so she could smoke.

Daniel took care of Melissa and gave her everything she wanted. He helped her enroll in school to get her GED. He asked her to marry him and have a child one day. He read various books and preached to Melissa daily about having good health. Melissa was not allowed to smoke or consume any alcohol. Daniel constantly talked about elevating their life.

After 2 years of living with Daniel, Melissa was exhausted and tired from all of his rules. She felt as if he was forcing her to abandon her family. But Daniel told her that the neighborhood they grew up in was a bad influence and they didn't need to be there.

Daniel had been trying to reach out to Melissa's brother, Joseph, for over a year. Daniel didn't understand why Melissa couldn't reach him. She would tell him because Joseph thought he was better than everybody. Daniel and Joseph were close growing up and he just wanted to have a conversation with him. He was confident he could repair Melissa and Joseph's relationship. Daniel was a family-oriented person who thought that family should be able to forgive one another and get past anything.

Another year passed and Melissa and Daniel were now married, Daniel invited Melissa to the Dominican Republic for their honeymoon. He told Melissa she needed to get her passport. He was persistent about it as the trip was four months away. Melissa began the process of getting her passport. She was excited to leave the country for the first time.

A week later, Melissa found out she'd been denied. Daniel asked her why she had gotten denied and she claimed she didn't know why and it didn't make any sense to her either. Daniel remained calm, kissed her, and promised he'd find a solution. He searched for different resources to help Melissa get her passport. But what Daniel found out why she couldn't get it. It caused him to lose his cool. Daniel found out Melissa had been imprisoned and had multiple charges of drug possession and intent to distribute. Not only that but Melissa owed $77,808.23 in child support. He did even more research on Melissa's past because now he knows about Mitch and Mike.

Daniel confronted Melissa about the drug convictions and her twins. She began crying uncontrollably and told him she didn't know how he would take it! Melissa explained that she got pregnant at 17 years old with Mitch and Mike. Daniel was in juvenile and a couple of months later, her son's father went to prison for capital murder and was doing a life sentence. Shortly after that, her moma's house was being foreclosed. She needed money, so she started delivering cocaine and heroin to Louisiana, Oklahoma, and Arkansas.

Daniel kept his calm posture as usual. He didn't ask any more questions but just sat at the dining room table and listened to Melissa. One could see the steam brewing from his head. His eyes were turning red as he held back his tears. When Melissa was finished explaining, Daniel got up from the dining room table, grabbed his hat, and left the house.

Daniel left for a whole week. Melissa got bored and caught the Greyhound bus back to her moma's house. Her youngest brother Dylan was sitting outside on the steps when she sneaked up on him in the backyard. Dylan was scared straight and fired his nine-millimeter pistol at Melissa. She was thankful the bullet missed her and shattered the car windshield instead. Melissa threw her bags on the ground and ducked behind the trash can. One of Dylan's friend, Josh, heard the commotion, and he came outside the house with a semi-automatic gun. Melissa yelled from behind the trash can with her hands up, "It's me, Melissa. Stop shooting!"

When Dylan recognized Melissa, he ran to hug her and threw her in the air. They were the most blissful moments she'd experienced in the last year. Dylan walked Melissa to the detached garage in the back of their house that he'd turned into his bachelor's pad. Josh had a bottle of Apple Crown Royal and poured everyone shots. Dylan pulled back a car cover, and beneath it was at least 100 pounds of marijuana and cocaine. He told her he had taken over their small town and delivered and sold drugs to other cities. While staring at Melissa's glistening, shiny rings, Dylan asked Melissa if she would help him or if she was a square like Daniel now. Melissa looked down at her engagement and wedding ring while twisting it around her finger. Finally, she took the ring off and told Dylan she was down for whatever!

Dylan and Josh poured more shots of Crown, and they drank until the bottle was empty. Drunk, Melissa asked Dylan where their moma was. Dylan and Josh looked at each other, and neither said anything. Then Dylan nodded his head and said she was in the house.

Melissa went inside the house. It was filthy. Her moma never kept the house in such a manner. Melissa stepped over the empty milk cartons, beer bottles, and soda cans. There were trash bags stacked on each other in the kitchen corner and ripped up books and magazines. As she went down the hallway, there were holes in the wall from someone punching it from anger. Her moma's glass table was crushed, and glass was in the middle of the floor. Finally, she made it to her moma's bedroom. She opened the door, and her eyes immediately came to tears when she saw her moma lying there helpless with an oxygen tank over her face. Her room smelled like urine. Melissa walked over to her and sat next to her in the bed. Her moma didn't move, but her eyes did. She didn't know what had happened to her moma. She'd only been gone for a couple of years.

Melissa lay silently in the bed next to her moma as tears ran down her face. The television was on her moma's favorite television show, "The Golden Girls." Melissa picked up her cell phone to call Daniel, but it went straight to voicemail. She didn't know how to handle her emotions. She was high off of weed and drunk on Crown Royal, and the thought of seeing her moma like that made her enraged. Melissa saw the bottles of medication on her moma's nightstand. She took several oxycontin. She laid back down next to her moma until she fell asleep.

Three days later, Melissa was awakened by Dylan screaming at her. She felt crappy when she got up and told Dylan to leave her alone. Her head was spinning and she felt nauseous. But Dylan insisted that she got up because he needed her to make a delivery to Arkansas. Grouchy, Melissa yelled at him, but he pulled her out of bed and told her in a stern, authoritative voice, "Get your ass up, or you will never get up again!"

Melissa got out of bed and wiped the crust from her eyes. She put her shoes on and walked to the garage to meet Dylan, who waved his nose. He told Melissa to take a bath because she smelled like dry shit and spoiled milk. Josh put his shirt over his face and agreed with Dylan. Melissa walked back into the house and went to the bathroom. It appeared as if it hadn't been cleaned since she left. The tub was black from mold and had a dark brown tinted ring around it. The sink was full of hair and blue gel shaving cream matted to the sides. There was a small amount of bleach under the sink, so Melissa cleaned what she could. She couldn't find a clean towel to take a bath, so she used a clean shirt she bought from Austin and washed her armpits, coochie, and ass. She rinsed her mouth out with a bottle of mouthwash because there wasn't any toothpaste.

An hour later, she went back to the garage where Dylan and Josh were. Dylan was upset because she'd taken too long. He gave her the address, and Josh threw the huge duffle bag at her. It was too heavy for her to lift, so Dylan put it into the trunk and handed her the keys to an old 1998 Buick. The trip was ten hours away. Melissa didn't have a driver's license and hadn't driven a car in over 12 years. But Dylan wasn't taken no for an answer, and Melissa needed money. She grabbed the burner phone, cranked up the car, and started on her way. The car's radio didn't work and duck tape held up the driver's window. Melissa did everything she could to entertain herself and stay awake. All she could think about was her moma and Daniel. Dylan explained to her that the doctor said she drank poison, but something about Dylan's story didn't make sense to Melissa. Then Melissa thought about Mike and Mitch's 16th birthday, which was coming up, and she wanted to see them. She was even more determined because she wanted to buy them birthday gifts.

It was midnight when Melissa made it to Arkansas. She begin dozing off as she drove. The burner phone was nothing like the new Iphone Daniel had gotten for her. She couldn't download Apple music, Youtube, or any other app to entertain her. Instead, she sang to herself as long as she could and planned to stop at the next exit so she could rest. As she exited the highway and headed towards McDonald's, she sped right past a state trooper. It was discreetly sitting between two large oak trees on top of a hill. Melissa saw him turn on his red and blue flashing lights and she hurried into McDonald's parking lot hoping to get away. But the officer pulled in right behind her and blocked her in the parking spot so she couldn't escape. The trooper walked to Melissa's car and asked for her license and insurance. Melissa didn't have either. He asked her why the car didn't have a license plate. She responded it was her brother's car. The law enforcement officer requested Melissa to step out of the vehicle while his partner called for backup. He asked if there were any drugs or weapons in the car, and Melissa told him no. The troopers began searching the vehicle while Melissa sat on the curb, handcuffed. They popped the trunk, and the officer pulled out a large black duffle bag. He asked Melissa what was in the bag. She said she didn't know. The officer nodded to his partner to search the bag. They found ten kilos of cocaine and fetanyl. They mirandized Melissa and put her in the back of the police SUV. She pleaded with them explaining she didn't know it was there or whose it was.

The judge gave Melissa 84 months in state jail and 5 years parole. Her defense attorney wanted her to snitch on Dylan, but Melissa refused. While she was in jail, she became a trustee and worked in the kitchen, so one day in jail was equivalent to 3 days. After three months, she'd gotten sick and was vomiting every morning. The smell of food caused her to be nauseous. Melissa couldn't work for four weeks, affecting her time served. Finally, she went to the infirmary and found out she was pregnant. Melissa didn't know who to call for help, so she didn't say anything to anyone. After she gave birth to her baby girl, Aria, the state took her baby girl. Melissa called Dylan for help for the first time since she had been in jail. Dylan informed her that their moma had passed a couple of nights ago.

One day, Daniel ran into Joseph at an annual block party in their hometown. Joseph introduced Daniel to Melissa's twins, and told him that she was a deadbeat mother. Then Joseph asked Daniel why he hadn't reached out to check on his two-month-old daughter, Aria. Daniel was shocked because he had no idea. He hadn't spoken to Melissa since he left almost a year ago. Daniel and Joseph exchanged numbers and decided to meet up at a local restaurant the following day.

The next day, Joseph begin by telling Daniel that he'd gotten all of his messages, but when he found out he and his sister were married, he stayed as far away as possible. He told Daniel that Melissa was a drug addict and drug dealer, and that's why he had custody of her kids their whole life. And that their moma spent over $250,000 hiring lawyers and admitting Melissa to drug rehabilitation programs to help her but nothing seemed to work.

A few weeks later, Melissa received a letter from the State of Texas stating that Daniel was filing for full custody for Aria. Of course, there wasn't anything Melissa could do about it. Her sons were about to be adults now, and she hadn't seen them in over a decade. Now she sat behind bars again, helpless.

Thirty six months later, Melissa was released from prison early with a fresh start. She went back to her moma's house, where Dylan and his wife, Natalie, lived with their nine-month-old son. Dylan was a fork-lift driver for a warehouse, and his wife did home health care. They allowed Melissa to live there, but they both agreed that she had to get a job. Melissa got a job working at Jack in the Box a week later, a block away from their house. She hated her job, but it was the only thing she could rely on.

Joseph, Mike, and Mitch came to visit Melissa. Mike and Mitch were both over six feet tall and bigger than her. She began to cry like a newborn baby. She wondered about Daniel and Aria and where they were. Joseph informed her that Daniel had gotten remarried, went back into the U.S. Marines, and moved to Germany. They stayed for twenty minutes before leaving. Melissa walked them to the car and hugged Mitch and Mike for as long as possible. Joseph rushed them to get into the car. Melissa stood on the curb and waved as they drove away.

She sat on the stairs in front of the house. She didn't know when she would see them again. Melissa started walking down the street, and noticed an average height, a slim, black man, getting out of a Chevy SUV. She locked her eyes on him. He must have felt Melissa watching him because he turned around, smiled, and asked, "What's good?" Melissa approached him and introduced herself; all she smelled was the pungent aroma of marijuana. She said, "I see you got that good!" His face lit up, and he got shy all of a sudden. Melissa continued, "So you gone fire me up or what?," trying to be charismatic and sexy. He stepped back and looked at her up and down, so Melissa turned around so he could get a better look at her full figure. He licked his lips and said, "Yea, you can come on in!"

Melissa went inside with him. His name was Richie, and you could tell he was a single man by his place. He had a 70-inch plasma television screen on the wall with a love seat, and he used sheets for curtains. Richie began tidying up the place by picking up clothes and shoes. Melissa asked him if he lived alone, and he told her he lived with his cousin, Mighty. Melissa and Richie stayed up all night watching reality television shows till 4:00 am. Melissa fell to sleep on the couch. Richie carried her to his bed. They cuddled all night until Richie tried to have sex with Melissa. Melissa let him have all of her. She didn't have anything to lose. When they were done, she saved Richie's number in her phone and told him they should do it again one night and she left for work. She purposely left her earrings on his dresser to ensure he would call.

An hour after Melissa arrived to work, Richie sent her a text message saying, "Hope to see you soon. Have a great and wonderful day!" Melissa knew she had Richie right where she wanted him. She didn't text him back but continued working. Richie called Melissa three days straight, but she never responded. One morning while Melissa was at work, Richie came through Jack in the Box drive-thru with his cousin, Mighty. She acted as if she didn't know him but took his money to complete his order. Richie said, "So you can't call nobody back?"

Melissa lightly blushed and gave Richie his change, saying, "I been busy, I will hit you later." She turned back around and gave them their food, and Richie sat there and stared at Melissa. She said with an attitude, "Did I forget something?"

Richie responded, "Yes! You forgot to call me back!" He smiled and drove off.

When Melissa got home later that night, she found out Natalie had lost her job and wrecked her car while on the way home. Rent was due in a couple of days. Melissa, Natalie, and Dylan sat around smoking and pondering how to get some money quickly. Melissa decided to hit Richie up that night. When she arrived to his house, Mighty was leaving with some girl. Richie passed her the joint as she walked inside. They sat on the couch and binged - watched MTV's Catfish. Richie gave Melissa a Four Loko, and they smoked joint after blunt after joint. Melissa observed all of the traffic that came in and out of Richie's house and the large sums of cash he collected. Although it was Melissa's second time around Richie, she knew he would do anything for her. Hungry, she wanted to test Richie's reaction when she told him. So Richie ordered some Chinese food from Door Dash.

From then on, Melissa visited Richie every day when she wasn't at work and scoped everything at his house. She was tired of her job, and Natalie hadn't found a job yet, so things were tight. One night while she was with Dylan, he'd explained that his son was sick and needed to be admitted to the hospital, but he had no insurance. The hospital kept sending him home. Melissa had an epiphany. She told Dylan and Natalie about Richie's large amount of money, and she knew where he stashed it. Melissa knew Richie would be home alone tomorrow night because she overheard Mighty say he would be helping his girlfriend move into her apartment. They decided they would rob Richie.

Natalie and Dylan got away with over $15,000 that night. Melissa didn't go because she knew he would recognize her. Dylan expressed that he had to get aggressive with Richie and knocked him out with his pistol. A week after the robbery, Melissa finally reached out to Richie after he'd called and texted her many times, urgently asking her to come over. Melissa finally visited him. She wanted to cry when she saw the large purple lump on his head and black eye. The house was trashed. Richie asked her why she had been avoiding him, and she told him she had to go out of town for a family emergency. Mighty came from the back room, and they started telling Melissa what happened during the robbery. Melissa didn't know what kind of behavior to expect from Richie, but she comforted him the best she could. She hugged him and told him she was sorry that it had happened to him. Richie assured Melissa he would be okay. Then he said to her that he owned a hair salon that his sister and aunt operated for him. Things would be challenging, but he had other ways to make money. Melissa held Richie's hand as they sat on the couch. He asked her if she would stand by him until he got back on his feet. Melissa promised she would.

It didn't take Richie long to get back on his feet. Before Melissa knew it, he had large stacks of cash again, and he'd purchased a rental property. She'd practically moved in with him. Dylan and Natalie hadn't given her any of the money they'd stolen from him. She was still stuck at her janky job. So Melissa told Richie she was pregnant and quit working at Jack in the Box. Richie loved the idea of Melissa living with him and being pregnant with his child. Although Melissa wasn't pregnant, she'd planned on getting pregnant real soon.

The Bottom of It All

It was Shelly's senior year in college at Texas A&M University. She and her roommate, Destiny, had been sharing a two-bedroom apartment for a couple of months, but it felt like forever. Shelly and Destiny became best friends instantly. They attended all of the University's sports games, ate breakfast together, and went out as often as possible.

Destiny's boyfriend, Xavier, was a Texas A&M graduate and had accepted a job back in his hometown Alabama. But he came to visit whenever he got two or more days off. Initially, Shelly did not like him the first few times he visited. Xavier was an arrogant, pretty boy who thought he was better than everyone. Xavier was always correcting Shelly's grammar, and his feet would stink up the entire house. Shelly didn't know what Destiny saw in Xavier, but she'd expressed to Shelly that she loved him and wanted to spend the rest of her life with him.

Destiny visited Xavier sometimes too, and Shelly went with her several times. At First, Shelly couldn't stand the thought of going to Alabama. But when she met Xavier's hippie mom, she made them her homemade chocolate edibles and rice crispy treats. Shelly decided she would tolerate Xavier for a bit longer. The more Shelly saw the two of them together, the more she could see them getting married. But on the other hand, Shelly wasn't the relationship type but liked keeping her options open. She'd dated so many people that they nicknamed her "Playgirl!"

It was Friday night and Ring Dunk weekend at Texas A&M. Destiny and Shelly received their Aggie Rings and hosted the biggest party in the history of the university. They invited all their neighbors and warned them that things might get loud. Shelly's best friend, Nathan, from high school, confirmed he was coming from the University of Texas in

Austin. Shelly couldn't wait for the night. She hasn't seen Nathan in over three years since the Texas Relays. They didn't speak much but kept in contact via Facebook. Shelly heard Nathan had changed a lot, and she couldn't wait to see him.

A few hours passed, and Shelly went to the bus station to pick Nathan up. She was running late as usual. The plans were to meet at the diner at the end of the street. But Shelly didn't see Nathan, so she patiently waited in the car near the bus station. Shelly watched as people walked past her. They tried to sell her pies, bottles of water, jewelry, weed, and other accessories. She didn't pay them any attention because she was distracted by a guy with short pink hair, a shiny dazzling purple shirt, and coochie cutter shorts. He stood in the middle of the street doing tricks with a black hat. It was weird, but the guy was talented. Shelly looked in her purse so she could tip him a dollar. As Shelly looked down, the guy twirling the black hat in the middle of the street approached her car. He tapped on the driver's window and said, "It's about time!"

Shelly then realized the guy was Nathan when he waved his hand. Another guy came around the corner with his baggage. She didn't know who he was, but he opened the trunk and began to put his luggage in the car. Both guys got into Shelly's car, and Nathan asked if she could drop his friend off somewhere. Shelly agreed while trying to focus on the road and observe Nathan from head to toe. The makeup on his face matched his clothes. His toenails were painted lavender. He'd definitely changed from high school.

In high school, Nathan expressed to Shelly that he liked her, but he liked guys, also. But Shelly wasn't expecting his appearance to completely change. Nathan asked Shelly how she'd been, but she replied with short answers because Nathan's friend gave her directions. Shelly had so many questions for Nathan. As bad as she wanted to converse with him, she didn't know what to say. So she just drove.

Shelly and Nathan made it back to her apartment. Destiny was almost done setting up the party decorations. Shelly joined Xavier in the kitchen, preparing the food and alcoholic beverages. Before Shelly could introduce Nathan, he appeared out of nowhere and began announcing himself. He made his way around the room and introduced himself to everyone.

Nathan spoke to Xavier, but Xavier turned and walked away. This made Nathan more dramatic and showed his flamboyant personality. Nathan asked Xavier if he was afraid of a proud faggot. Again, Xavier didn't say anything but looked at Nathan distastefully. Shelly grabbed Nathan and took him to the bedroom. He expressed to her that he didn't feel comfortable around Xavier. She admitted that Xavier was a little different, and she didn't like him at first, but he eventually grew on her. But Nathan didn't take that for an answer. Instead, he told her he would get to the bottom of it. Shelly persuaded Nathan to leave it alone. But he was persistent about finding the real issue Xavier had with him. Shelly knew he wouldn't let it go, so she left it alone and walked away.

Meanwhile, Nathan got into the shower to prepare for the party. Shelly went back into the living room area to check the party's status. Xavier pulled her aside and asked if they could talk on the patio. Shelly agreed and just knew it was about Nathan. When Shelly and Xavier reached the balcony, he reached into his pocket and pulled out a jewelry box. He opened it, and there was an enormous diamond ring. Xavier wanted to propose to Destiny during the party and wanted to know what Shelly thought. She told him it was a great idea and Destiny had been waiting for this day her entire life.

While Shelly had Xavier's attention, she wanted to address Xavier's problem with Nathan. Xavier replied that he just didn't like Nathan's type and wanted him to stay away from him. Shelly and Destiny dunked their rings in a pitcher of beer and chugged it as fast as they could until they reached their rings. Everyone at the party cheered them on. Xavier nervously walked out of the kitchen getting ready to propose to Destiny, he ran into Nathan and Nathan wasted his drink all over himself. They got into an altercation disturbing the party and Destiny and Shelly had to get in between the two of them. Xavier was calling Nathan a bunch of racial slurs. Nathan told Xavier he wasn't a real man. They had to keep them on different sides of the room the entire night.

Later that night, everyone was drunk and high on weed and pills. Destiny was passed out on the couch. Shelly tried multiple times to wake her, but she was out of there. Shelly looked for Nathan, but she couldn't find him. It was odd because an hour earlier, he was the life of the party but now missing in action. As Shelly walked through the house looking for Nathan, she began picking trash up from around the house. It was 3:00 AM, and most guests were starting to leave. Shelly's good friend, Roman, stayed late to help her clean. They laughed at how Destiny had gotten engaged and partied too hard. People continued leaving, and Roman asked Shelly what she thought about Xavier and Destiny getting married. Shelly replied that she liked Xavier and thought he was a good and just right for Destiny. Roman just shook his head and asked me where Xavier was since Destiny was passed out on the couch. Nearly everyone had left. Shelly and Roman couldn't find Xavier or Nathan.

After cleaning up the living room and kitchen, Shelly's head began spinning. Roman asked her if she needed to smoke. He pulled out his stash and a pack of backwoods. Before he fired up the blunt, he went to the bathroom. Shelly recommended he use the one in her room because it was clean.

Moments later, as Shelly was firing up the back wood, Roman suddenly rushed back around the corner with a confused look. He'd looked like he'd seen a ghost.

Shelly joked and asked him if he was okay. Then she handed him the back wood because it seemed he needed to smoke more than she did. Roman didn't say anything. He waved his hands and told Shelly to come here. Shelly became concerned and followed him to her room and the bathroom. Everything seemed normal. Shelly didn't know what had Roman acting that way. Then Shelly heard a crackling sound coming from the closet in her bathroom. It caught her by surprise because she had never heard the sound before. Then she heard moaning, and Roman opened the door and told her to go inside. Shelly peeped her head into the closet. She saw Nathan bend over with his pants down around his ankles, and Xavier's pants were down to her knees. He was humping Nathan like a dog. Shelly stood there frozen in the closet until Xavier saw her standing there. He jumped back, pulled his pants up, and said, "It's not what you think!" Shelly replied, "I guess you did get to the bottom of it."

All in the Family

When Elise was 14, her parents were killed head-on in a car collision. She had four older siblings, but the State of Texas wouldn't allow her to live with any of them. Originally from Dallas, Texas, Elise was forced to reside in Vicksburg, Mississippi with her dad's parents.

Elise hated being in Mississippi. It was nothing like Dallas but had many narrow one-way roads and fields of crops. The city of Jackson was the only place to go out and hang with friends, shop, and party. It was 45 minutes away from Elise's grandparent's house. She didn't have a car but didn't go out either. She was aware of what everyone was doing because she would overhear the other kids at school talking about parties on Monday morning.

Elise was 6 feet, weighed 175 pounds, had pure muscle, and presented masculine energy, so most of the guys were intimidated by her. She was a tomboy, wore baggy clothes, and kept her hair braided in cornrows to the back. Elise's grandma would slander her for looking like a boy, so she just started wearing her hair in an Afro or a bushy ponytail instead of braids. On Saturday nights, Elise's grandma stayed up late to press her hair with a straightening comb. Her grandma forced her to wear dresses, pantyhose, and heels to church. Elise hated it.

One day, Elise's grandma decided she would begin shopping for Elise's clothes. She wanted her to dress more girly. But Elise found a way around this. She would tell her grandparents she was staying late for tutoring at school, but instead, she would go to the mall and steal clothes from the boys' section. Elise got away with it for a few months until her grandparents had to bail her out of jail for theft.

By the time Elise was a senior in high school, her grandparents had bailed her out of jail seven times for theft. Elise had been expelled and sent to an alternative school, but she decided to drop out. After she dropped out, her grandparents evicted Elise from their home. Elise wondered what her older siblings were doing. She'd lost contact with them after leaving Texas. Other than her grandparents, Elise had one contact on her prepaid cell phone. A girl's name was Samantha. Samantha was a few years older than Elise and lived with her boyfriend, Marvin, in an apartment in Edwards, Mississippi. It was about twenty minutes away from where her grandparents lived.

Elise met Samantha while doing community service several months ago for probation. Samantha always complimented Elise on how she wore her natural afro and even shared her food. Samantha pleaded guilty to a drug case over two years ago. She went to jail for 90 days, had to serve probation for 5 years, and performed 200 hours of community service. One night while Samantha was on her way to pick Marvin up from one of his boys' houses, a Sheriff pulled her over because she was speeding. The officer saw weed residue in the middle console, searched her vehicle, and found an ounce of weed and a couple of grams of cocaine. Samantha went to jail and paid Marvin back for the drugs.

Elise was skeptical about contacting Samantha because Samantha invited her to her birthday party a few weeks ago, but Elise didn't go. She thought it was a setup because she felt people wished the worst for her. But Elise had nowhere else to go, no money and only three minutes left on my prepaid phone. So she decided to call Samantha anyway.

Samantha answered the phone and immediately asked, "Who is this?"

Elise waited to respond because Samantha didn't sound like herself. She thought she had the wrong number. Then Samantha yelled through the phone, "Who the fuck is this?"

Elise knew it was Samantha, but she sounded angry while crying. Elise wanted to hang up the phone but finally replied, "Elise! Elise from community service!"

There was a sudden silence as if Samantha had walked away from the phone. Then Elise heard a sniffle, and Samantha said, "Hey, girl, what's up?"

"Are you OK?" Elise asked Samantha. Samantha got quiet again, and there was an awkward silence.

Samantha's boyfriend, Marvin, was never home. Elise knew because Samantha always complained about him being gone while they were doing community service.

Elise's prepaid phone immediately warned her that she had one minute left. She quickly got to the point and asked Samantha if she could come to pick her up and if she could stay at her house for a few nights. Samantha quickly agreed then the call disconnected.

Forty-five minutes later, Samantha arrived. Elise put her two large, black trash bags full of clothes and tennis shoes in the backseat, and they drove off in Samantha's 97' Chevy Suburban.

The two of them arrived at Samantha's apartment. Elise was intrigued with her 60-inch television hanging from the wall because she didn't watch TV at her grandparent's house. They had an old black and white floor TV in their bedroom. Samantha told Elise to make herself comfortable, which is precisely what Elise did. It was cozy and the air conditioner was blowing cold at 65 degrees. Samantha's refrigerator and freezer were full of food, and the pantry was packed with all kinds of cakes, candy, and chips.

Samantha approached Elise with two shot glasses and a bottle of 1800 tequila. Elise hadn't had anything to drink since she was 12 years old when her mom bought her dad a bottle of whiskey for his birthday. Elise didn't know what whiskey was then, but the glow in her dad's eyes when he saw it made her want to try it. Elise planned to get my hands on that bottle for months to get a taste. Finally, one weekend her parents went to a church convention. They left Elise at home with her older sister Janice. Janice's boyfriend came over, and they were upstairs in her room all night. Elise made it a mission to get the bottle of whiskey and she did! At first, she thought it was disgusting. The drink burnt her mouth and chest. She couldn't breathe. She took another sip to see if she would get the same reaction. It still burnt her tongue, but it didn't burn as bad. She took another and a few more until she finally couldn't taste it anymore. She began feeling buzzed. The things in her parents' closet were circling her. Shed fell asleep. When her dad came home and saw she'd drunk all of his whiskey, he was hysterical and punished her until she was 18 years old.

Samantha relentlessly took her two shots and handed one to Elise. Then poured them another one. Elise tried to drink her shot as quickly as Samantha did, but that was a huge mistake because it came right back up and landed all over Samantha's kitchen floor. Elise gave her puppy dog eyes, hoping she wouldn't be mad, but instead, Samantha started laughing and called her a "rookie."

Samantha grabbed some pineapple juice from the fridge, mixed 1800, and told Elise to drink it, and she did. They stayed up all night drinking and discussing their lives. Samantha confessed to Elise that she walked in on Marvin and one of her best friends having sex. She explained that the three of them had sex together sometimes, but she never thought the two of them would go behind her back.

Elise felt lousy for Samantha but enjoyed her vulnerability and honesty. As Samantha talked, Elise checked out her dark red, long curly hair, and she had the body figure of a 20 oz soda bottle, and her ass moved like a wave in the ocean when she walked. Elise had never been intimate with anyone before. She had been questioning her sexuality since the third grade when she realized she was in love with her math teacher, Ms. Chi. Now Elise was starting to feel the same way about Samantha. These feelings made it clear what Elise wanted. Around 4 AM, Elise grabbed a blanket and fell asleep on the couch. Samantha got under the blanket, lay next to Elise, and started spooning with her.

A month had gone by, and Marvin came and got the things Samantha packed up for him. The bag had been sitting near the front door for a few weeks. Marvin apologized 100 times for his actions and begged Samantha to forgive him. He even got on his knees. Elise sat on the couch observing while eating a bowl of Cinnamon toast crunch. Samantha didn't say anything or even look up at Marvin but waved her hand for him to leave.

Over time, Samantha and Elise became best friends, and Elise could tell her anything. She told her about her parents being killed in a car accident and how her grandparents gave up on her. She didn't have any contact with her older brothers and sisters. But Samantha took care of Elise, paid all of the bills, cooked for her, and they even had sex regularly.

After three years of Samantha and Elise being together, Samantha started complaining about wanting more from life. She told Elise she needed to get a job and make her own money, so she could buy her stuff sometimes. This frightened Elise. She didn't even know where to start looking for a job. She didn't even graduate from high school. Elise promised Samantha she would look for a job the next day. But the next morning, Elise awoke with a stomach ache and complained she couldn't get out of bed. She was sick for two weeks. Samantha threatened to take her to the hospital but Elise refused to go. She suddenly got better.

Elise played it cool for a few days. She continued lying around the house, hoping Samantha forgot about her getting a job and things would go back to normal. Samantha continued nagging; before Elise knew it, she was cooking only for herself. She stopped washing Elise's clothes and cleaning up behind her.

The following week, Samantha told Elise that a guy contacted her through social media claiming to be her father, and wanted to meet with her.
Samantha didn't know anything about him. Her mom would always shut down when she questioned her about her father. Elise agreed to go with her to meet him. So Samantha messaged him back they agreed to meet the following day.

When Samantha and Elise made it to the restaurant, Samantha was shaking and sweating so hard that all the curls in her long dark red hair were now straight. Elise held her hand and tried to calm her by reminding Samantha how perfect she was. Elise told her he had no reason not to like her and continuously held her hand as they waited for him.

As they waited, the waitress came to their table multiple times, anxious to take their order. But Samantha insisted they wait on her dad. An hour went by, and Samantha's dad still had not arrived. Her shirt was soaked with sweat. She was ready to go home, but Elise was starving, so she placed her order. Her food arrived 30 minutes later. Elise offered some to Samantha but she refused to eat and replied that she had no appetite so Elise finished it. Elise knew Samantha was disappointed her dad didn't show. So she ordered her favorite feel-good food, strawberry cheesecake, but Samantha didn't want it and pushed it to the side, so Elise ate it. Then this short, muscular curly-haired man wearing skinny jeans and a hoodie approached their table. He spoke softly and said, "Sam, baby girl?"

His arms were open as if he'd missed her, and he continued, "You are just as beautiful as you are in your Facebook pictures."

The man hugged Samantha, and she hugged him back. Elise could see Samantha sigh in relief. He joined them at the table and introduced himself as Michael Perry. Elise shook his hand, and the waitress came back over. Michael expressed he was starving and exhausted from catching all the buses to the restaurant. He ordered a medium-rare steak with lobster, chicken strips with a loaded baked potato, and a bottle of the restaurant's best champagne.

As Michael sat at the table, he explained he'd gotten fired from his job, so he thought it would be the perfect time to meet Samantha. Samantha and Elise stayed at the restaurant for two more hours listening to Michael complain about how bad life was. The waitress handed the check to Michael. He glanced at Samantha while reaching for his wallet in many different places on his body. Then he asked Samantha if she could take care of it because he was low on cash. Without a doubt, Samantha paid for everyone's dinner. She even paid for Michael to get an Uber to return to his motel.

When Samantha and Elise returned home, they showered and began getting ready for bed. Samantha was so excited to meet her dad for the first time. She couldn't stop talking about him. Elise didn't like him, but she didn't tell Samantha that. While in bed, Samantha opened her laptop. She'd received 16 new messages from Facebook. All from her dad. He messaged her that the motel had given his room away, and he had nowhere to stay the night. Samantha told Elise then Elise confessed to her she didn't feel right about him and that he was just using her. Samantha got offended and told Elise that she could leave her house if she didn't like it. So Elise kept her mouth shut. Samantha paid for her dad another Uber to come to her house. An hour later, there was a knock at the door, she allowed him to stay in the guest room.

Michael lived with Samantha and Elise for two months. He didn't cook or clean up after himself but laid around the house all day, smoking weed, and drinking all of Samantha's tequila. Things were becoming stressful for Samantha. One day Samantha and Elise got into a heated argument, and Samantha left for two days, and no one could reach her. Elise didn't know what to do without her. Michael nor Elise had any money or knew how to cook, so they just smoked and drank all day. They wished she would come back and they made a toast to their big happy family.

Mr. Perry and Elise conversed all night. He told Elise he had 16 kids, and Samantha was the oldest. Her moma had her when she was 15 years old. Around the same time, Michael had impregnated three other women. He told Elise he got everything he wanted because he knew how to lay the dick down! Therefore he didn't have to do anything else.

After a few more drinks, Michael asked Elise if she'd ever had sex with a man. Elise replied that she hadn't and told Michael she didn't like men. She continued saying she was in love with Samantha and had been since the first time she saw her. Michael insisted that Elise couldn't know she didn't like dick unless she tried it. Elise debated with him that she could miss something she'd never had before. Michael moved closer to Elise on the couch and told her sex was natural between a man and a woman and that she didn't have to be afraid. He pulled out his penis, grabbed her hand, and stroked his stiff dick up and down. After a few moments, Michael let go, and Elise continued. Michael asked Elise if she wanted to kiss it. She stared at it and thought about it but then shook her head saying no. He took his right hand, put it under her shirt, and rubbed her left nipple.

Elise sat relaxed on the couch with her hand still stroking Michael's large erect dick. Then Michael softly started kissing her on her neck, doing swirls with his tongue. Elise's legs began to shake as he lifted her shirt and started sucking on her left breast, now reaching his hand down her sweatpants. He gently rubbed her clitoris while using the other hand to finger her. Elise's eyes rolled into the back of her head as she slouched down on the couch even more.

Elise stood up, and she was so wet it felt like she peed on herself. Michael hurriedly pulled down her sweatpants and stuck his penis into her vagina. She resisted at first. She screamed and tried to run. But as Michael penetrated her, he whispered in her ear, "Everything was going to be OK."

Elise wanted to tell him to stop, but it felt good. He continued kissing her on her neck and inserted one of his fingers into her booty hole while penetrating her vagina. Elise had an orgasm like she'd never had before. When they were done, they both lay on the couch naked, temporarily relieved from their stress. Then Elise was awakened by Samantha standing over the two of them. Her eyes were bloodshot red, her face was pale, and she held a butcher knife in her right hand!

The Pastor's Side Chick

It was Mother's Day, a Sunday painted with vibrant blues and greens as flowers bloomed around Houston. The church service came to a close, leaving the congregation buzzing with chatter and laughter. Dajuana, however, felt the familiar void within her. With no children of her own and her mother passed away five years ago, the day was bittersweet. She didn't even know why she went to church that Sunday.

Dajuana's stomach grumbled, reminding her that she hadn't eaten anything all day. Craving comfort food as only Liby's could provide, she headed there for dinner. As she approached her car, the sun glinted off the windshield, and the warm air wrapped around her like a gentle embrace. To clear her mind and indulge in a moment of nostalgia, she lit up a Backwood and took a deep drag of the smooth, earthy flavor infused with some of Houston's finest weed. The smoke curled out of the window as she leaned back, letting her worries dissipate for a moment.

When Dajuana finally stepped inside the restaurant, it was packed. The line was outside the doors, an unyielding crowd eager to savor the last day of Luby's. Dajuana's mouth watered at the thought of their famous meatloaf and crispy fried fish, and she decided to wait.

After standing in line for nearly thirty minutes, her mind wandered again, but it was interrupted by a lively voice from the man in front of her. He was dressed sharply in a striking red suit that hugged his lean frame, and his black shiny snakeskin shoes gleamed under the fluorescent lights. The other gentlemen noticed his hat and complimented him on his bold choice, but the guy had his eyes only for Dajuana.

"Hey there, I just have to say—you smell incredible," he remarked, a friendly grin spreading across his face.

Dajuana felt the heat rise to her cheeks, a flurry of embarrassment washing over her as she realized he noticed the scent of the weed lingering on her clothes. "Oh, um, thanks!" she replied, trying to hide her bashfulness behind a small smile. "I, uh, just came from my car."

"Nothing wrong with that. Gotta unwind, right?" He chuckled, his charm disarming her. "I'm Dru, by the way."

"Dajuana," she replied, extending her hand for a shake.

His grip was warm and firm, instantly making her feel more at ease. "Nice to meet you, Dajuana.

He asked what brought her into the restaurant.

Dajuana replied, "Just craving some meatloaf. Today's the last day for this place," she explained.

"Me too. I couldn't let this opportunity pass. Luby's is legendary," Dru said, nodding thoughtfully. "Their fried fish is unbeatable!"

Dajuana laughed, the sound lifting her mood. "Exactly! And the meatloaf! I'd do just about anything for it right now."

They continued chatting as the line slowly inched forward, finding a rhythm in their conversation. Dajuana learned that Dru was from out of town, but recently opened a church in 5th ward Houston.

As the line shuffled along, the atmosphere felt lighter, almost festive. Dajuana felt a connection sparking. She hadn't expected to meet someone like Dru on a day that had started so heavy on her heart.

Dajuana stepped out of Luby's, her mind swirling with thoughts of Dru. The pastor had a presence about him that drew her in, a warmth that made her feel seen—something she hadn't felt in years. After three years of celibacy, she found herself captivated, wondering if he might be the man she had been waiting for her entire life. His faith, strength, and gentle smile resonated deeply within her.

She hesitated at her car, gripping her keys tightly. The thought of letting this chance slip away was unsettling. Determined, she turned around and went back into the restaurant, her heart racing. There he was, still chatting with a few members of the congregation. Gathering her courage, she approached Dru, her heart pounding.

"Hi again," she said, her voice steady despite her nerves. "I realized I'd like to get to know you better." She grabbed his phone. He looked surprised but pleased as she entered her number.

"I'd love that," he replied, a smile lighting up his features.

As Dajuana walked back to her car, she felt a flutter of hope. Just as she settled into the driver's seat, her phone buzzed with a message from Dru: "Hey, it was great to meet you! Looking forward to talking more."

A smile crept across her face. She quickly typed back, "I got you," feeling a spark of excitement at the prospect of connecting with him.

Upon arriving home, Dajuana ate her meal and her mind still racing with the possibilities of her and Dru. After eating, she felt her eyelids growing heavy so she took a nap. She drifted off, and thoughts of Dru continued dancing behind her eyelids.

A few hours later, she awoke to her phone buzzing again. This time, it was Dru inviting her to his church that evening. "I'm preaching tonight. Would love to see you there," he added his church's flyer.

Dajuana hesitated. She had already been to church that day and felt a mix of reluctance and fatigue wash over her. But as she pondered the invitation, a thought struck her—someday, she might be the First Lady of this church. While she was in this position, she'd need to be present, always supporting her husband's ministry.

Taking a deep breath, Dajuana realized this was an opportunity she shouldn't miss. "I need to get used to this," she murmured to herself. With renewed determination, she texted Dru: "I'll be there."

After a quick shower and putting on her favorite dress, Dajuana felt a sense of purpose enveloping her. As she drove to the church, she reflected on how her life was beginning to change in ways she never expected. The buzz of anticipation resonated in her as she envisioned the possibilities of her future with Dru, a man whose faith and commitment to God inspired her in ways she had only dreamt of.

Pulling into the church parking lot, she took a moment to collect herself, praying for guidance and clarity. Tonight, she would not only support Dru; she would explore the beginning of something remarkable. As she stepped out of her car, she felt ready to embrace whatever God had in store for her.

Dajuana had always been curious about the church on the corner of Maple and Cedar. The sound of drums and laughter spilled out on Sunday mornings. Today, she had finally decided to step inside and see for herself what the buzz was all about.

The congregation stood, hands raised, completely engrossed in the moment, and that's when she spotted him: Dru. He stood confidently at the pulpit, a magnetic presence that drew her in like a moth to a flame. He preached with passion, his voice rich and melodic, effortlessly captivating everyone in the room. Dajuana felt her heart race; he was everything she had ever dreamed of in a man—charismatic, articulate, and undeniably gifted.

As the service progressed, Dru transitioned from preaching to music, his hands gliding over the piano keys with elegance. Dajuana watched in awe as he moved to the saxophone. He then picked up the drums, leading an energetic beat that had the congregation clapping along enthusiastically. It was as if he were a modern-day prophet, connecting everyone in the room with his extraordinary talents.

Hours slipped by, and Dajuana found herself swept away in a haze of admiration. Yet, as the intensity of the service continued, fatigue began to tug at her eyelids. She tried to fight it, but the warmth and soothing rhythms lulled her into a gentle doze. After three hours, she realized it was time to leave; the last thing she wanted was to be caught snoring in the front row.

She quietly slipped out the side door, hoping to sneak away unnoticed. But as she crossed the threshold back into reality, a voice came through the mic, clear and unmistakable: "We thank you for being here today, and to the lovely lady who just left, I hope to see you again!" Dajuana froze mid-step. Did he just acknowledge her? Heart racing, she hurried to her car and drove away.

Once home, she took a long, relaxing shower, the warm water washing away the day's emotions and energy. But her mind remained fixed on Dru—the way he commanded the room, his infectious smile, the way he played with such passion. She felt an undeniable connection even though they had barely spoken.

As she wrapped a towel around herself, her phone buzzed insistently on the counter. She grabbed it, a flutter of excitement coursing through her veins—there was a missed call from Dru!

Without a second thought, she hurriedly dialed his number, her heart pounding with anticipation.

After a few rings, he answered, his voice smooth as silk. "Dajuana, is that you?"

"Yes, it's me!" she replied, a mix of nerves and elation bubbling within her.

"I noticed you in the crowd today. I hope you enjoyed the service."

She smiled, her cheeks flushing. "I did! You were incredible up there."

"Thank you," Dru said, laughter lacing his words. "I was hoping you would come to Galveston with me this weekend. I'd love to see you again and I'm preaching.

Dajuana stared at her bank account with a frown. She'd just paid her rent including late fees. Her funds were barely enough to cover essentials, let alone a trip to Galveston. She wanted too badly, but she knew she had to decline the invitation.

Her phone buzzed, lighting up with a message from Dru. "Hey! Are you still coming to Galveston this weekend?"

For a moment, she hesitated before typing back. "I don't think I can make it. Money is really tight right now."

To her surprise, Dru replied almost instantly. "No worries! I booked a three-bedroom Airbnb. I can cover your gas as well."

Dajuana's heart raced at the thought. It was so generous of him, and the idea of spending time together at the beach thrilled her. "Are you serious? I'd love to go!"

"Great! Just get here whenever you can," he responded.

As the day progressed, however, Dajuana knew she wouldn't be able to make it until later that night. She had to work late.

Finally, when her shift ended, she rushed home to pack a small bag—a bathing suit, a carefree sundress, and her favorite sandals. She quickly jumped in her car and hit the road. It was an hour-and-a-half drive. Her heart racing at the thought of seeing Dru.

The sun dipped below the horizon when Dajuana arrived at the beach house. Dru stood outside, his face lighting up as he spotted her. "You made it!" he exclaimed, coming over to greet her with a warm hug. She couldn't help but breathe in his fresh scent as they embraced, feeling a spark of connection.

"I'm sorry I missed your sermon," she said, pulling back slightly to look him in the eye.

"No worries. I'll fill you in later," Dru said with a playful wink. "But first, I have a surprise for you."

"Another surprise?" she asked, intrigued.

"Yup! I thought we could kick off the weekend with dinner at your favorite place—Landry's. How does that sound?"

Her eyes widened with delight. "That sounds perfect! I love their seafood!"

With that, they headed to the restaurant. Sea salt wafted through the air, mingling with the scent of fried fish and grilled shrimp. The ambiance was vibrant—families gathered for celebrations, couples enjoying cozy dinners, and the gentle sound of waves crashing against the shore filled the background.

They settled into a corner booth, and Dru ordered a platter of oysters, shrimp, and crab. As their food arrived, they chatted eagerly about everything from music to their dreams for the future. Dru was everything she had felt during that first encounter—passionate, interesting, and deeply engaging.

Over dinner, Dajuana felt as if she were floating, the world beyond their table fading away. The way Dru spoke about life, love, and purpose captivated her, and she found herself motivating him to share more about his sermons and passions.

After they finished eating, Dru suggested they take a walk along the beach. The moon hung low in the sky, casting shimmering reflections on the water. They strolled side by side, the soft sand beneath their feet, and the sound of the gentle waves created a soothing soundtrack for their budding connection.

"Have you ever considered doing something beyond preaching?" Dajuana asked. "You have so many talents."

Dru chuckled softly. "Sometimes, I think about it. Music is my first love, but I feel a calling to connect with people in a deeper way."

"I can see that in you," she replied, glancing up at him. "You have a way of making people feel valued."

They stopped a little way down the beach, gazing out at the water. Dajuana felt a warmth spread through her as Dru turned to her, the moonlight illuminating the kind eyes that held her gaze.

"You know, I'm really glad you decided to come. It's nice to have someone who truly understands."

A blush crept to her cheeks, and she replied, "I'm glad too. I almost didn't come."

"Life has a funny way of working out, doesn't it?" Dru smiled.

They went back to the Air Bnb and Dajuana was ready to shower after a long day. Dru told her he had some phone calls to make while she was showering. Dajuana gave him an okay and took a hot, steamy shower. As she was drying herself with the towel, Dru heard her and immediately wrapped up his phone call. Dajuana asked him if he was okay because he was acting strange but he assured her that he was fine as he laid on the bed.

As the night went on, Dajuana realized that this trip would become a cherished memory—the beginning of something beautiful with Dru. It was more than just a getaway; it felt like a stepping stone toward a future filled with possibilities. While Dajuana and Dru lay in the bed entwined, the passion between them intensified. Dajuana's curiosity about Dru's penis had been piqued, and she wanted to explore every inch of him. With a playful glint in her eye, she traced her fingers along his body, her touch sending shivers down his spine. Their kisses deepened as Dajuana's exploration continued, and Dru couldn't help but let out a soft moan of pleasure. The room filled with the sounds of their desire.

The chemistry between them was electric, and their connection seemed to transcend the physical. As their intimacy progressed, it felt as though they were creating their own little world within the confines of the Air BnB. Time seemed to stand still as they lost themselves in each other.

The passion between them built to a crescendo, and as they reached the peak of their pleasure, it felt as though their souls were intertwined. At that moment, nothing else mattered—the world outside ceased to exist. Dajuana and Dru had found solace and comfort in each other's arms, and as they lay together afterward, a sense of peace and contentment washed over them.

The next morning, they were awakened by the harsh, insistent ringing of Dru's phone. It was 5:00 AM, a time most people were still asleep. Dru glanced at the screen, squinting against the glare from the open window. The name flashing was one he recognized but didn't quite expect: Wife.

With a groggy swipe, he declined the call, convinced it was just another one of those early morning conversations that could wait. He settled back into the warmth of his covers, wrapping his large body across Dajuana, trying to slip back into sleep as the distant sound of birds began to fill the air.

But within minutes, the phone buzzed again, breaking the peaceful silence. This time, it was a text message from Wife: "Dru, it's urgent. Call me ASAP."

A knot formed in Dru's stomach. He sat up slowly, the weight of impending news pressing on him. He hesitated for a moment. Maybe his wife just needed a ride or just to talk. But something told him it was more serious.

The phone rang a third time, louder and more demanding than before. Dajuana told him to answer it because it must have been an emergency. Dru's heart raced as he ran out of the bedroom. He knew he could no longer ignore it. He took a deep breath and answered.

His wife was calling to tell him that his son had been in a car accident while he was traveling. Dru rushed back into the room and quickly put on his clothes. Dajuana asked him if everything was okay. He told her he had to leave. It was an emergency. Before she could respond, Dru was out the door, each step feeling like a desperate attempt to outrun the darkness that threatened to close in around him.

Dajuana sat at her kitchen table, staring at her phone with a mix of frustration and concern. It had been a week since Dru had rushed out of the AirBnb.

After days of trying to reach him, Dajuana couldn't shake the feeling that her calls were being forwarded. Each attempt to connect was met with silence, and each voicemail she left felt like a plea lost in the void. "Dru, please call me back. I just want to hear from you," she said in her last message. But still, nothing.

Determined to find him, she turned to Facebook, hoping for a hint of where he might be or what he was up to. She scrolled through her feed, her heart sinking at every post that flashed by. Finally, she found his profile, and there it was a post announcing that he would be preaching that night at a local church.

Dajuana's heart raced. She called her job and told them she would not be making it to work that night, it felt like destiny. She wanted to see him, even if it was only to understand what had happened.

As the day turned to dusk, Dajuana picked out her best outfit—a soft, white dress that flowed gently around her knees, paired with a light cardigan. She adorned herself with the silver necklace her mother purchased her before she passed. Standing in front of the mirror, she rehearsed words she hoped she would get to say: "I miss you, and I'm here for you."

Arriving at the church, she felt a mix of excitement and apprehension. The soft hum of chatter welcomed her as she stepped inside. The sanctuary was filled with warmth and the glow from overhead chandeliers illuminated the joyful faces of friends and family. But where was Dru?

Dajuana took a seat in the middle row, her heart beating steadily as she observed the congregation. She fidgeted with her necklace, glancing at the door, waiting and hoping he would walk in. The service soon began, and the music floated through the air, but her thoughts were consumed with worry. Where is Dru?

As the pastor welcomed everyone and shared the announcements, Dajuana's attention shifted to the pulpit. Suddenly, she spotted Dru. He emerged from the side, a presence of strength and calm. His eyes scanned the room before settling on her—and for a brief moment, the world around him faded.

Dru nervously stepped up to the microphone but instantly was able to get himself back together, he greeted the congregation. He wore a crisp white shirt and a navy blazer, his hair had a fresh fade. He smiled as he began to speak, but Dajuana sensed something was off. His words flowed, but they felt heavy with unspoken thoughts, almost like a shield he wore against the vulnerability of the moment.

"Good evening. I want to talk about faith during difficult times," he began. Dajuana could hear the sincerity in his voice, each word propelled by his earnest desire to uplift those in attendance. She listened attentively, even as her heart ached for him.

"The past week has been challenging for so many of us, including myself. Life has a way of throwing unexpected trials in our path—testing our strength, our patience, and our faith. But what we must remember is that we are never truly alone."

Dajuana's heart constricted at the weight of his words. She knew the struggles he faced, but she felt more isolated than ever, longing to reach out to him. He continued, weaving in personal anecdotes, sharing stories of resilience and hope, but she could still see the shadow behind his eyes.

After the sermon, Dajuana approached Dru as he greeted members of the church, her heart pounding. When he saw her, he smiled, but it didn't erase the concern etched on his face.

"Dajuana! I didn't know you were coming," he said, his tone warm, yet laced with hesitation.

"I've been trying to reach you all week," she replied, her voice steady as she stepped closer. "I was worried. You disappeared."

Dru looked down for a moment, then back at her, vulnerability shining through. "I'm sorry. It's been overwhelming. I've been... processing everything. Work, family, life—it all just caught up to me. I should have reached out."

Dajuana nodded, her heart aching for him. "You don't have to go through this alone, you know. I'm here for you. Whatever you need."

He nodded, gratitude shining in his eyes. "I appreciate that. I didn't mean to shut you out. I just... didn't want to burden you with my struggles."

Dajuana took a step closer, closing the physical distance between them. "You could never be a burden to me. But shutting me out feels like a bigger burden. Let me help you."

Suddenly, out of the corner of his eye, he spotted a familiar figure approaching. Dru's heart sank as he recognized the unmistakable silhouette of his wife, Effie. She walked gracefully, her long hair cascading over her shoulders, oblivious to the emotional exchange happening a few feet away.

"Dru!" she called cheerfully, her smile bright and welcoming. "I'm so glad I found you. I have someone I want you to meet."

Dru's stomach twisted as he turned to face her. He felt a moment of panic. He didn't want to introduce his wife to Dajuana at that moment. It felt too complicated. But before he could make sense of the situation, Effie was stepping closer.

"Who's this?" she asked, curious as she glanced at Dajuana.

"This is Dajuana, a friend from the community," Dru replied, his heart racing as he attempted to maintain composure.

Dajuana extended her hand with a polite smile, her heart pounding. "Nice to meet you," she said, though the words felt hollow as confusion washed over her. Inside, she felt something shift, a prickling sensation nudging at her intuition as she made the connection. How could Dru have a wife?

Effie beamed, shaking Dajuana's hand, but her gaze lingered on Dru, searching for an explanation. "Oh, that's wonderful! We love having new faces in the church!"

Dajuana forced a smile, but the air felt heavy with unspoken tension. "Yes, I'm glad I could come tonight," her voice wavering slightly.

Dru shifted uncomfortably, sensing the sudden strain in the atmosphere. He had wanted to keep Dajuana's support separate from his marital life, but fate had other plans. "We—um, we were just talking," he said, fumbling with his words. "I'm really grateful for her support."

There was a moment of silence, and Dajuana felt a rush of panic. Support? The word echoed painfully in her mind, clashing against the reality that unfolded before her. She thought they were forging a deeper connection, but here was Effie, a reminder of Dru's life that he hadn't fully shared with her.

"Sounds great!" Effie replied cheerfully, but the smile on her face didn't reach her eyes. Dajuana's heart raced as she processed what was happening. She felt abruptly out of place, like a puzzle piece that didn't quite fit.

"I... I should go," Dajuana stammered, the words tumbling out before she could think them through. Without another word, she turned on her heels and rushed toward the exit, her heart pounding in her chest.

Dru watched helplessly as she hurried out the door, his body frozen in place as a wave of regret washed over him. He glanced at Effie, who looked genuinely puzzled.

Dajuana reached her car, fumbling with her keys amid the storm of emotions swirling inside her. She slipped into the driver's seat and slammed the door, her breath coming in rapid bursts. As she leaned against the steering wheel, tears streamed down her cheeks unbidden.

How could he have a wife? How could he have let her believe there was something more between them? She pressed her forehead against the steering wheel, feeling the weight of betrayal and sadness wrap around her.

As she composed herself, the sound of her heartbeat echoed in her ears. She wanted to scream, to cry out in frustration and hurt. It was as if the safety net she had felt just moments before had been ripped away, leaving her exposed. She felt foolish for believing that their bond could become something deeper, something meaningful. But now she was faced with the dark reality of Dru's life—his family, his commitments.

After a few moments of solitude, she wiped her eyes and took a deep breath. She couldn't let this tear her down; she had to regain her strength. Maybe this was a sign—a moment to refocus on herself.

Deep down, Dru knew it would take more than words to mend the situation he had unintentionally created. He quickly took his phone out, desperate to call Dajuana and apologize. He had to make her understand that their connection didn't have to be complicated. He reached out, determined to set things right.

The night stretched on, dark and heavy, as Dru sat on the edge of his bed, staring at his phone. He felt like he was in a whirlwind, emotions swirling chaotically within him. After the encounter at church, he couldn't shake the sinking feeling in his chest. Dajuana had left so abruptly, and the look of confusion on her face haunted him.

Determined to reach her, he dialed her number again. Each ring felt like a countdown, each unanswered call deepening the pit of anxiety in his stomach. "Please pick up... please," he whispered to himself, frustration mixing with concern.

After a few missed calls, Dajuana finally answered, her voice a mix of anger and hurt. "What do you want, Dru?"

"Dajuana, I—" he began, but she cut him off.

"I can't believe you. After everything we talked about, you just... you just shut me out! You have a wife, Dru! You didn't feel the need to tell me that before you invited me to Galveston?"

"It's not that simple," he implored, desperate to explain his feelings. "I never wanted to hurt you. You mean a lot to me."

"Don't you dare say that!" she shot back. "You think that makes this all okay? I thought we were building something real, something special, but I'm just a secret! I hate you for lying to me, Dru!"

"I didn't lie," he said softly, his voice low. "I just didn't know how to tell you. Everything happened so fast, and I—I didn't want to hurt you. You are someone I can truly love, Dajuana. You deserve to know that."

There was a pause on the line. Dru's heart raced as he waited for her response.

"What do you mean?" she finally asked, her voice softer now, tinged with confusion. "What are you saying?"

"I'm saying that I've been thinking about my life, about my marriage... and I'm considering leaving Effie," he confessed, his voice trembling. "I haven't been happy for a long time, and I see a future with you Dajuana."

Dajuana felt her heart skip a beat. She had imagined this moment but never truly believed it could happen. "Are you serious?" she asked.

"Yes. But I need you to understand that this is complicated. Leaving Effie would be a big step, but I can't ignore what I feel for you."

For a moment, silence enveloped them again as Dajuana processed what Dru said. "And how do you expect me to believe that you're not just saying this because you feel guilty? You've built a life with her."

"I know," he replied, his voice thick with emotion. "But my heart is with you. I want to be with you. I want to figure this out—together."

Dajuana took a deep breath, her emotions in turmoil. She felt anger, confusion, and hope. "What if this is a mistake? What if you end up regretting it?"

"It won't be a mistake," he said firmly. "I'll regret staying in a marriage where I'm not fulfilled. I want to come over tonight. We need to talk in person."
"Dru..." she began, but he interrupted.

"Please, let's just talk. I need to look you in the eyes and tell you how I truly feel."

After a moment of hesitation, Dajuana finally replied, "Fine. But if this turns into more confusion, we're done. I can't handle any more hurt."

"I understand. Thank you for trusting me," he said, relief flooding through him. "I'll be there soon."

When Dajuana opened the door, the intensity of her gaze sent a shiver down his spine. She looked beautiful but vulnerable, the soft light from inside reflected the uncertainty in her eyes.

"Dru," she said, her voice steady yet laced with emotion. "We need to be honest tonight. No more games."

"I agree," he said, stepping inside and closing the door behind him. "I'm here to be completely open with you."

They moved to the small living room, their usual comfort in each other's presence now tinged with tension. Dru took a deep breath as he sat down across from her. "I know I've hurt you, and for that, I'm truly sorry. But I want a life with you. I want to understand what we could be together."

Dajuana looked at him, her heart battling between the hope of a future and the fear of the unknown. "And what does that mean for Effie? For your marriage?"

"I don't know," he admitted, his voice raw with honesty. "Her father invested in me and bought me four churches across the state of Texas. I have to figure it all out. But I can't pretend to be happy anymore. I want to choose happiness, and right now, that means being with you."

Tears welled in Dajuana's eyes as she listened, feeling the weight of his words wash over her. "What if this is a mistake—what if we're just reacting to the situation?"

Dru leaned forward, his gaze unwavering. "I can't ignore how I feel about you, the connection we have. You make me feel alive; you see me for who I am—beyond the titles of husband, pastor, or whatever else I've tried to be."

Dajuana wiped at her tears. "You're still married, Dru. This isn't just about us; it affects everyone."

"I know," he replied, his voice steady. "But I can't deny my feelings. I've been living a life that doesn't reflect who I want to be. If we step forward, I just need you to promise that you will wait on me until I figure it out.

There was a heavy silence as they both took a deep breath, the enormity of the decision weighing on them. Dajuana felt swept up in a whirlwind of hope and trepidation. Their chemistry was undeniable. Could she really give in to this connection, knowing it could change everything?

"Dru," she said softly, "if we do this, we have to go all in. No second-guessing, no turning back."

"Agreed," he replied, his expression earnest and unwavering. "I want to choose this, to choose you. If there are consequences, I'll face them."

They sat together in the silence that followed, a spark ignited between them—an unspoken understanding that they were on to something new and beautiful.

Dajuana leaned closer, her heart racing. "Okay, then. Let's see where this takes us. But know that I'm not someone to be taken lightly. If we're doing this, we need to put everything on the line."

Dru kissed Dajuana softly and she kissed him back.

Are you sure?" Dru asked, his voice barely above a whisper, filled with reverence.

Dajuana nodded, "I've never been more sure of anything in my life."

With that, they closed the distance between them, their lips meeting in a soft, tentative kiss that quickly ignited into something deeper. His hands cradled her face gently as if she were the most precious thing in the world. Dajuana melted against Dru's body, sinking into the warmth of his embrace, feeling safe and desired.

As their kisses deepened, a feeling of urgency washed over them. Dru lifted her, cradling her against him as he led her to the bedroom. Everything felt right. It was as if they were two stars colliding, destined to shine brighter together.

Once they reached the bedroom, Dru laid her down gently, taking a moment to drink all of the juices that excreted from her. The soft light illuminated her features, making her look ethereal. "You're so beautiful," he murmured, leaning down to capture her lips once more.

Their bodies moved together, melding in perfect harmony. Nothing mattered at that time— there were no worries, no guilt, no past. Just this moment. Dru's hands explored Dajuana's body, feeling the curves that drove him wild. She responded to his touch like a flower blooming in the sunlight, every caress igniting flames of passion deep within her.

Their bodies entwined, moving together with a rhythm that felt instinctual, as though they had danced this dance many times before. It felt like a reunion, a coming home. Dajuana surrendered herself completely, allowing Dru to lead the way.

Their breaths quickened, hearts pounding as they lost themselves in one another. With every kiss and every touch driving them closer to the edge. They locked eyes, and in that shared gaze, they found a connection deeper than any words could express.

"Dajuana..." Dru breathed, his voice thick with intensity.

"I'm right here," she replied, their hearts beating at the same pulse.

As they approached that peak, an overwhelming wave of pleasure surged through them. They felt each other's bodies tighten, the world around them no longer existed. With a final thrust, they climaxed together, a passion that echoed in the stillness of the night. In that climactic moment, everything crystallized—their desires, their fears, and the love that had grown between them despite all odds.

They lay entwined after, breaths mingling in the quiet of the room. It was a blissful, euphoric haze, and Dajuana couldn't remember ever feeling so alive. "That was... everything," she whispered, a satisfied smile gracing her lips as she lay against Dru's chest.

"Yeah," he replied softly, his fingers tracing patterns on her skin. "You're incredible."

In the days that followed, Dajuana tried to reach out to Dru, but all of her calls went unanswered again. Each time she listened to the familiar sound of his voicemail, her heart sank a little further. It was as if he had vanished. Their passionate night felt like a dream.

At the clinic, Dajuana sat nervously in the waiting room, tapping her foot anxiously. The doctor finally called her in, and she took a deep breath as she entered the examination room. After discussing her health and general concerns, the doctor suggested a pregnancy test due to a sudden awareness of hormonal changes.

Dajuana felt a rush of anxiety as she took the test. When the doctor returned, a smile on her face.

"We have good news," the doctor said gently. "You're pregnant."

Dajuana's world tilted on its axis. A flood of emotions washed over her—joy, fear, confusion, all at once. She tried to process the implications, but the reality sent her thoughts reeling. Would Dru even want this?

She felt so alone in a moment that should have been filled with support and joy. She had tried to reach Dru so many times, and now this?

After leaving the clinic, Dajuana sat in her car, staring blankly at the road ahead. She felt the enormity of her situation weighing heavily on her shoulders. Suddenly, thoughts of Dru flooded back. He was the one she wanted to share this with, the one she had been vulnerable with—if only he would answer.

Gripping the steering wheel tightly, she felt the sting of tears in her eyes. She wanted to reach out to him, but what if he didn't want to know? What if he wasn't ready for this kind of responsibility?

With a heavy heart, she took a deep breath and resolved to give herself some time. Whatever was meant to happen would happen; she just had to be strong enough to face it—alone, if necessary.

Dajuana couldn't shake the memory of their time together, the way they connected, the love she felt. As she drove home, she clung to a flicker of hope.

Dajuana had spent those lonely weeks trying to reach Dru, but each call had gone unanswered. She even searched for his Facebook page countless times, desperately hoping to find a piece of his presence. But every effort turned up empty as if he had disappeared completely.

Despite everything that happened, Dajuana tried to move forward, focusing on her career and self-care. However, the absence of Dru weighed heart and mind heavily. She missed him—the conversations, the laughter, the chemistry between them.

One afternoon, as she prepared dinner in her cozy apartment, her phone buzzed unexpectedly. She looked down to see an unfamiliar number. Could it be? She answered with anticipation.

"Dajuana?" his voice came through the receiver, instantly recognizable.

"Dru!" she exclaimed. "Where have you been?"

"I've been... around. I needed some space to figure things out, but I've missed you. Can we meet?"

Dajuana hesitated. But the warmth in his voice melted her resolve. "Sure, when?"

"How about tonight? I'd love to see you."

Smiling to herself, she agreed and quickly made plans. "I'll cook something nice. You'll love it."

As the sun began to set, Dajuana set to work in the kitchen, as she prepared a home-cooked meal for Dru. She cooked salmon with a drizzle of lemon garlic sauce, served with asparagus and quinoa.

Before long, the doorbell rang, and Dajuana opened the door. Dru stood on her doorstep, a soft smile on his face, and her heart fluttered at the sight of him. He looked good, a little more worn but somehow still the same man she remembered.

"Wow, it smells amazing in here," he said, stepping inside.

"It's just a little something I threw together," she replied bashfully, leading him to the dining table where she had set candles and flowers to create a romantic atmosphere.

As they sat down to eat, laughter and conversation flowed easily between them as usual. But beneath the surface of their reunion, she knew she needed to tell him about the surprise she had been keeping—a moment she had both anticipated and dreaded.

After dinner, as they cleared the table, Dajuana took a deep breath. "Dru, I have something important to tell you."

He looked at her curiously, a playful spark in his eyes. "What is it?"

"I'm pregnant," she blurted out.

The smile on Dru's face faded instantly, replaced by a look of disappointment that cut through Dajuana like a knife. "Oh," he said, his voice dropping to a near whisper. "I see."

"I know this is unexpected," she continued, desperate to explain. "But I think this will bring us closer together."

An awkward silence hung in the air. Dru shifted uncomfortably in his seat, running a hand over the waves in his head. "Dajuana, I... I didn't expect you to say that."

"I understand if you're upset," she said quickly. "But we can talk about it. Like what to do next."

Dru shook his head slowly, confusion across his face. "Dajuana, I'm not sure how to handle this. I already have eight kids with four different mothers. I didn't mean for this to happen. I can't take on more right now."

Dajuana's heart sank, his words hitting her like a punch to the gut.

"I care about you! I wanted us to have a future, but another baby... I can't do it, not right now. My life is already complicated, and I've struggled to give my time to the kids I already have," he finished, his voice strained with emotion.

Her mind raced as she fought back tears. "So, is that it? You want me to just... to get rid of it? You don't want to be involved at all?"

"I don't want you to be upset, but I need to be honest. I can't support another child right now."

Suddenly, all of Dajuana's hopes for a happy reunion shattered. "I thought you were different."

"I care about you, Dajuana. A lot!" he said, urgency creeping into his tone. "But this—this can't happen."

Fighting against the tears that threatened to spill, Dajuana rose from the table, feeling suffocated by the their conversation. She turned away, trying to gather her thoughts, but all she felt was a disappointment and confusion.

"Dajuana, please," Dru said, standing up and moving toward her. "I never wanted to hurt you, but we have to think long-term."

She shook her head, not wanting to hear anymore. "I need time to think about everything," she said finally, her voice trembling. "I need space."

Dru nodded slowly, a defeated look in his eyes. "Okay," he replied quietly. "I'll give you that."

As he walked toward the door, Dru paused at the door, turning back to her one last time. "I'm sorry, Dajuana," he said. "I truly care about you, more than you know. I just... I can't be the man you need right now. I am asking you to please not keep this baby."

With that, he left, leaving Dajuana standing alone in her kitchen, the fading scent of the dinner she had prepared swallowing her. Tears streamed down her face as she sank onto a chair, with reality crashing down around her. She made the decision that day to do what was in her best interest and that was to keep their baby.

His Wife Overdosed

Michael was nearly 30 years old, a young entrepreneur who had built a successful trucking company in Little Rock, Arkansas. He prided himself on providing jobs for his community, employing five hardworking drivers who looked up to him.

Dana was just 17, fresh from a traumatic past. Moving from Detroit, Michigan, to Little Rock and a bumpy transition for her. The death of her mother was due to a heroin addiction. With her mother gone, Dana moved in with her Aunt Sally, hoping to find stability for herself and her two-year-old daughter, Moni. But life continued to throw challenges her way, and things got worse. One rainy afternoon, Dana got caught up in a tumultuous argument with her Aunt Sally about her curfew and responsibilities. Sally kicked Dana and Moni out on the streets.

With nowhere to go, Dana wandered with Moni in her arms, tears streaming down her face. Just when she thought she had reached the end of her rope, she bumped into Michael in a grocery store.

Initially, their interaction was brief. Michael noticed Dana's tired eyes and her frightened daughter. They exchanged smiles, but he felt drawn to her sadness. At that moment, he couldn't shake the feeling of wanting to help. It was then that he decided to approach Dana.

"Excuse me," he said in a friendly tone, finding her sitting on a bench outside the store. "I couldn't help but notice you looked like you could use a little help. Are you okay?"

Dana looked up, surprised by his kindness. "I-I'm fine," she stammered.

After a brief conversation, the truth came out. Michael learned about Dana's struggles, her mother's death, and the fight with Aunt Sally. He felt empathy for her situation. Without thinking too much, he offered a place to stay. "I have a spare room in my house. I can't just let you and Moni stay out on the streets."

Dana hesitated, uncertainty creeping into her mind. "Are you sure? I don't want to be a burden," she replied, biting her lip.

"Trust me, it'll be okay. I can help you get on your feet. You need a safe place for you and your daughter," Michael reassured her.

That evening, they arrived at Michael's two-story, four-bedroom house. The home was full and empty, you could tell Michael was a single man. He had no pictures on the wall. His refrigerator only had a protein shake and a carton of eggs. He promised Dana they could go to Walmart to get whatever she and Moni needed so they would be comfortable.

As days turned into weeks, Michael and Dana adjusted to their new living arrangement. Dana took care of Moni while Michael ran his company. They spent evenings getting to know each other. Laughter filled the house as Moni played.

Dana struggled to adapt to living with an older man and managing her responsibilities as a young mother. Michael did his best to create a comfortable environment but he felt Dana was wrestling with her feelings about their new relationship.

As the months passed, Dana started rebuilding her life. She enrolled in a local high school so she could get her GED. Michael helped her find affordable childcare for Moni. Moni cooked Michael home-cooked meals every night and ran him a hot bath. Their friendship blossomed into something deeper, a bond formed through shared experiences and understanding.

In time, Dana and Michael became inseparable. They learned to navigate their relationship. Michael respected Dana's independence, and Dana appreciated Michael's support and unconditional love.

Then there was Michael's younger sister, Shante. She was carefree and often experimented with drugs. She would sip cough syrup, smoke weed, and pop various pills then brag about her escapades. Dana found herself drawn to Shante's vivacious spirit. Their relationship grew and they would often hang out.

Dana faced a turning point when she began smoking weed. Michael disapproved. Seeking a way to still be around Shante, she shifted to popping pills like Xanax and Percocets.

At first, Dana relished the euphoric feeling. Michael began to notice her erratic mood swings and dwindling appetite, but Dana dismissed their concerns. She assured herself that everything was under control, that she could still handle being a mother to her daughter and a supportive fiancée to Michael.

One sunny afternoon, the trio visited the aquarium. Midway through their adventure, Dana suddenly felt faint. She collapsed onto the cool tiles, leaving Michael and Moni panicking.

When Dana came to, Michael's worry deepened as he looked into her eyes, searching for answers in the momentary daze of concern. As they headed home, he couldn't shake the nagging thought: was Dana using drugs?

That night, Michael decided to confront Shante. After all, she had become a regular presence in their lives, and he needed to know the truth. "Is Dana on drugs?" he asked.

Shante paused and quickly came to Dana's defense. "No way, Michael. Dana would never do that. She's a good girl," she insisted. She felt she had to protect Dana because she was one of her regular customers and would spend all of her money on pills.

As the days unfolded, Michael observed Dana's continued mood swings and disinterest in everything. Despite what Shante said, he felt desperate to understand the transformation in his fiancée.

With a heavy heart, he approached Dana. "Dana, I'm worried about you," he said gently, reaching out for her hand.

In a small town, Dana finally felt like she was entering a new chapter. Her relationship with Michael flourished, despite the challenges they faced in the past. A year after their tumultuous times, Dana discovered she was pregnant.

When news of the pregnancy hit, Michael was overjoyed. He dreamed of fatherhood and envisioned a loving family together. As the months rolled by, their anticipation grew, and they began preparing for their little one's arrival. Friends and family offered their support, but not everyone was happy for the two of them.

Michael's mother, Evelyn, was always skeptical about Dana. She didn't like her son's choice of partner and openly expressed her discontent. She often made sideways comments about Dana's past and questioned her suitability as a mother.

Despite Evelyn, Dana remained positive. The pregnancy blossomed into a beautiful journey, and on a sunny day in June, she gave birth to a healthy baby boy. They chose the name Michael Jr. But everyone quickly picked up on his nickname, June Bug, which suited his playful spirit.

All the joy and love that filled their new family unit made the outside criticism seem distant. However, Evelyn's discontent was hard to ignore. When she first met baby June Bug, her icy demeanor intensified. "You could have a much better life, Michael," she suggested. "You don't need to settle for Dana."

But Michael stood firm. He loved Dana, and his commitment to her and their son was unbreakable. "Mom, I'm not going anywhere," he replied. "I want to be here for my son and Dana. She is his mother, and we're building our family together."

Evelyn frowned. "You're young. You could have kids with someone more... suitable. Someone who will elevate you," she retorted. Michael's refusal to abandon Dana made her even madder.

Michael persisted in showcasing his love for Dana, wrapping his arms around her during late-night feedings and laughing over diaper disasters.

As Thanksgiving approached, the scent of sweet potato pie, and the anticipation of family gatherings. Michael was busy planning the holiday with Dana. Excited for their first Thanksgiving as a complete family with June Bug and Dana's daughter Moni.

Michael was on a route training one of his new truck drivers. His phone rang, causing his heart to skip a beat. The number on the screen was from the hospital.

"Hello, this is Michael," he answered, trying to keep his voice steady.

"Mr. Boone, I'm calling from the hospital. We have some urgent news regarding Dana," the voice on the other end said. Michael's heart sank. "We found her in her car in the parking lot of her job. She was unconscious. Firefighters had to break the window to get her out. We administered two doses of Narcan to revive her. She's now stable, but we need you to come down here."

"What do you mean, 'unconscious'?" he stammered, his mind racing. Michael immediately turned the 52″ truck around and headed back to the yard. He grabbed his keys and headed to the hospital.

Arriving at the hospital, he was met with the anxiety that filled the sterile environment. After what felt like an eternity, a doctor finally emerged, giving Michael an overview of Dana's condition. "She's recovering, but you should know that she'll be facing legal consequences. Two police officers are currently at her bedside."

Michael's heart sank further at the thought. "What do you mean legal consequences?" he asked, already dreading what he might hear next.

"They found substances in her system that indicate driving under the influence," the doctor replied. I will let one of the officers know that you are here and they can better explain.

Stunned, Michael struggled to process the information. "I have our son June Bug and Moni with me. What am I supposed to do?" he asked, feeling overwhelmed.

Micheal pulled out his phone and called Shante.

"Shante, I need your help! It's urgent," he said. "Dana's in the hospital. They found her unconscious in her car, and they charged her with DUI. I can't do this alone sis."

"I'm on my way!" she exclaimed. Within a short time, she arrived at the hospital. "What happened?"

Michael filled her in. Feeling the weight of the situation pressing down on him. "I have the kids, but I don't know how to manage everything. Dana's in trouble, and I need to be there for her, but I can't leave the kids?"

Shante nodded, "Okay, let's take it one step at a time. I can help with the kids. I will pick them up from school today."

With Shante's support, Michael felt a glimmer of relief. He rushed to Dana's hospital room, his heart racing.

When he entered, Dana lay in bed, looking fragile and pale, her eyes flickering open as she took in the scene. A police officer stood nearby, waiting for her to regain full consciousness. "Michael..." she murmured.

"Dana, what happened?" he asked, "Are you okay?"

She nodded slowly, "I don't know.... I'm so sorry, Michael."

Michael held her hand, "You scared me, Dana. June Bug and Moni are with Shante."

The police officers stepped forward. "Dana, we need to inform you that you are under arrest for DUI."
Looking up at Michael, "What am I going to do?" she whispered.

Michael squeezed her hand, "We'll figure this out together. Focus on your recovery."

After the officers left, Dana looked at Michael, "I never wanted to hurt our family. I'll change, I swear," she said, her voice trembling.

"I believe you, Dana," he replied.

Dana overdosed on pills just the night before. She'd bailed herself out of jail. Not wanting to return home just yet, she booked a room at a nearby hotel.

Later that night, Dana arrived back home after being gone for two long days. Moni and June Bug were happy Dana was back home. Tears began to run down her face as Dana rejoiced to be back home. She looked at Michael while holding her children tightly and she whispered, "I'm so sorry for everything. I want to change."

"You have to go to rehab," he stated, his voice gentle yet firm. "It's the only way we can move forward."

Dana nodded, "I agree. I'll go."

The following morning, Dana checked into a rehabilitation center, ready to confront her addiction head-on. For five days, she immersed herself in group therapy, counseling sessions, and the difficult process of self-reflection. But Thanksgiving was coming up and she wanted to be home with her family.

After her DUI, her life had taken an unexpected turn, leading her to probation. Michael loved Dana and was going to do anything he could to support Dana. He wanted to solidify their family. So they got married at church. Michael's mother did not attend.

As time passed, the weight of her probation began to feel like a shackle. Dana was required to attend NA meetings and check-ins with her probation officer once a week. But Dana struggled to give up her old party habits. She convinced herself she could manage both worlds—her marriage and her desires.

One day, while Dana was attending a mandated community service, she met Elijah. He was charismatic and magnetic, he had lots of tattoos and his mouth was full of gold. Elijah didn't judge her. Instead, he was intrigued by her wild spirit. They hit it off instantly. Elijah booked a motel one night and Dana had sex with him. When she was with Elijah, she felt a sense of freedom—a freedom that included the drugs he gave her.

As the weeks passed, Dana's nights became filled with wild parties and drugs. She would go to parties right after work and stopped going home. She spent more and more time with Elijah, who increasingly introduced her to a world of substances that clouded her judgment and numbed the guilt she felt about betraying Michael. While her husband worked to care for their family, Dana was busy living a life she knew was unsustainable.

One weekend, Dana told Michael she was traveling to Atlanta, Georgia to visit her best friend and maid of honor at their wedding. Michael agreed with her but he had doubts in his mind. He contacted their mobile phone company and had them locate her. The night took a turn into certainty. Driven by an instinctual need to protect what he cherished, Michael followed Dana to a hotel in Little Rock where they lived. He spotted her laughing and leaning into Elijah, their chemistry undeniable.

Michael confronted Dana, "How could you?" he asked. Dana realized she could no longer deny the consequences of her choices.

"I'm sorry! I'm so lost..." she cried, tears streaming down her cheeks.

"It's not just about us anymore, Dana. You need help," Michael replied, voice cracking. "I loved you."

As the weeks passed, they attended marriage counseling together. The sessions were challenging. Emotions ran high as they unpacked feelings of betrayal, insecurity, and love. Michael expressed his fears about trusting Dana again, while she openly acknowledged her struggles with drug addiction and the choices that led to her downfall.

Their counselor guided them through exercises that encouraged honesty and accountability. Slowly, the walls between them began to dissolve. After every session, they felt they were moving a little closer again and in tune with one another's emotions and experiences.

Dana also made an effort to reconnect with her faith. They attended church services regularly. Despite her commitment to change, Dana struggled to meet the conditions of her probation when the drugs clouded her judgment. She missed consecutive months of meetings with her probation officer. Her Probation officer made her admit to an inpatient drug rehabilitation center.

The reality of her situation hit her hard: thirty days of rehab. To atone for months of missed probation appointments and failed drug tests.

The more isolated she felt from the family she loved. But every weekend, Michael and the kids would visit come Dana.

As the weeks passed, Dana tried her best to focus on her recovery. She attended group therapy and individual counseling sessions, learning about the triggers that led her to substance abuse. However, she longed to return to the normalcy of her life.

One Saturday, as Dana sat outside with Michael and the kids, she noticed Moni was quieter than usual, and June Bug kept looking at her father searching for reassurance.

"Are you guys alright?" Dana asked, concern deep in her voice.

Michael sighed deeply, taking a moment before responding. "We're okay, but it's been hard, Dana. We miss you. The kids have been asking a lot of questions."

Dana's heart sank. "I know I've put you all through so much. I'm so sorry."

The day finally arrived for Dana to step out of the rehab facility and into her new life. After thirty days of hard work, self-reflection, and commitment to sobriety, she was excited but nervous at the same time.

When she arrived home, her heart raced with anticipation. The sight of her husband brought tears to her eyes.

"I'm so sorry, Michael," she whispered. "I've missed you and the kids more than I can express. I want to fix our family. I'm committed to doing whatever it takes."

"I'm just happy you're home," Michael replied, his voice reassuring. The love in his eyes sparked hope within her.

The weeks that followed were filled with adjustments and new routines. Dana was determined to prove she was serious about her recovery. She attended meetings, remained committed to her counseling, went to church, and focused on reconnecting with Michael, Moni, and June Bug.

One Sunday afternoon, Dana was home and grateful to be back with her family. However, she couldn't shake a growing sense of exhaustion that had settled in over the past few weeks.

As the weeks turned into months, Dana noticed that her fatigue hadn't subsided. One evening, after putting the kids to bed, Dana took a deep breath and decided to take a pregnancy test. As she waited for the results, anxiety took over her body. A few minutes later, she stood staring at the test, stunned. Her emotions swirled uncontrollably when she saw the unmistakable two pink lines. Dana was pregnant.

The Purity Thief

Trina was a senior in high school and had been in a relationship with her boyfriend, Mack, for two years. However, things were complicated; while they had previously shared a deep connection, Mack had recently been unfaithful multiple times. Trina, initially committed to waiting until marriage to become intimate, struggled to understand why Mack couldn't do the same for her.

Despite his constant declarations of love and his desire to spend the rest of his life with her, Mack insisted that his needs weren't being met in the relationship, which led him to cheat. Trina loved Mack deeply and longed for a strong connection with him. Finally, on prom night, torn between her feelings for him and her values, she decided to give him her virginity, hoping it would solidify their bond and reignite the love they once shared.

Trina's first experience was disappointing. She had watched porn videos before, and they were far more thrilling than the brief 2½ minutes Mack had just given her. Feeling unsatisfied and disheartened, she didn't want to continue. Mack seemed indifferent, lacking the intimacy she craved—there were no kisses or eye contact. Once it was over, Trina quickly put her clothes back on, sitting on the bed as Mack dressed, gave her a quick kiss on the forehead, and handed her money for an Uber before leaving.

Feeling unsettled, Trina reached for her purse and grabbed some ibuprofen. She felt cramps in her stomach and noticed blood on her underwear, causing panic to rise within her. Uncertain about what to do, she tried calling Mack to return to the hotel room, but each call went straight to his voicemail. In distress, she finally called her best friend Dion to pick her up from the hotel.

Trina got into the car with Dion and opened up about everything that had happened. As they drove around looking for Mack throughout the night, Dion grew increasingly upset. Despite Trina's repeated attempts to call Mack, he never answered. Dion, who had never liked Mack, voiced his frustration, calling him a dog and expressing how much he disapproved of him.

When they finally arrived at Trina's parents' house, Dion helped her inside, recognizing that she could barely walk. It was 4:30 AM, and her parents were still asleep. Before Dion left, he hesitated, then said, "I really didn't want to tell you this, but Mack has a child on the way." With that, he left.

Trina couldn't bring herself to believe it, though she had heard whispers at school about Mack possibly getting one of his band members pregnant. After a long, exhausting night, she took a shower and tried calling him one last time before settling into bed. As she lay there, her mind raced with thoughts about their future together.

A couple of weeks later, Trina and Mack graduated from high school, but they hadn't spoken since prom night. Mack was avoiding her at all costs; whenever she spotted him at school, he would quickly rush in the opposite direction. Trina tried calling him, only to find that he had blocked her number. When she stopped by his house, his mom and brother always claimed he wasn't home, despite his car being parked in the driveway.

Months passed, and Trina enrolled at The University of North Texas, discovering the freedom to be her true self. She dyed her hair red and began wearing form-fitting clothes, changing her name to "Chocolate Drip." In just a few months on campus, she had collected phone numbers from many of the freshmen guys and started talking to a quiet, shy freshman named Stephen. His innocence was evident, and Trina loved that she could take the lead in their relationship.

Trina and Stephen hung out for a while, but initially, it was challenging to get him to sleep with her since he was more interested in establishing a relationship. Eventually, she seduced him, and they became intimate. However, after taking his virginity, Stephen became clingy and controlling, prompting Trina to start avoiding him.

While on campus one day, she bumped into a guy named Jarod, whom she had met at a fraternity party. He asked her to lunch and expressed a desire to get to know her better. Jarod had the same innocent charm as Stefan, and Trina found herself drawn to him. Before long, she started inviting Jarod over to her dorm room —he was next on her list.

Initially, Jarod always brought along his friend, Allen. Together, they acted like typical teenage boys, which was a turn-off for Trina. However, Trina and Jarod went to lunch every day consecutive for two weeks. Her attraction to him grew. One day while Trina, Jarod, and Allen were in her dorm room, Trina asked them if they were virgins. Allen replied that he wasn't and had been with almost every freshman girl on UNT's campus. Jarod sat there with his head down and nodded that he was. Allen began pointing and laughing at him.

The next time Jarod came to Trina's dorm, he was unusually quiet. After about ten minutes of trying to figure out what was wrong, Allen finally admitted it. Reluctantly, he admitted that he felt embarrassed about the question she asked him. Trina laughed lightly, realizing his feelings were genuinely hurt. She reached over and kissed him on the cheek, but he quickly turned his head, hoping for a kiss on the lips. Unfortunately, they ended up bumping heads, which made them both laugh.

Once they composed themselves, Trina gazed into Jarod's eyes, feeling a spark. She placed her hand behind his head and leaned in, kissing him gently. Their connection intensified, and Trina slipped her tongue into his mouth. As they kissed, she pushed him down onto the bed and climbed on top, wanting to take the lead. Reaching into her top drawer, she pulled out a condom and began putting it on him.

She positioned herself over him, gently guiding him inside her. As she rode him, Jarod's eyes rolled into the back of his head. He moaned her name. A few minutes later, after they finished, Trina knew that she had him wrapped around her finger.

Later that night, Jarod mentioned that he wanted Trina to meet his mom and grandma. It was already 1:30 AM, and with an 8 AM class approaching, she knew it was time for Jarod to leave. He begged her to let him stay the night, wanting to cuddle, but Trina told him she had to go to a friend's house to drop off some medications. She began putting on her clothes. Reluctantly, Jarod said goodbye and left.

A week passed, and Jarod called Trina at least five times each day. Eventually leading her to block him. One day after class, she bumped into Allen, who seemed upset. Concerned, she asked him what was wrong. Allen told her that Jarod was a lil bitch and couldn't be trusted.

Feeling empathetic and wanting to know more, Trina invited Allen to her room, where she offered him a glass of grape soda mixed with Crown Royal to help him relax. She inquired about his falling out with Jarod. As he spoke, Trina gently rubbed his back to comfort him. Enjoying it, Allen took off his shirt and laid on the couch. Trina interrupted him while he was talking and asked him how it felt. Allen told her it felt amazing!

Then Trina began kissing him on his back, gently with each kiss down his back. Allen began squirming. He flipped over and you could see the huge bulge in his pants. Before he could say anything, Trina started, kissing him on the mouth and wrapped her arms and legs around his body while she sucked his tongue. She unbuckled his belt and stuck her hand down his pants. She wanted to feel the bulge and just as she expected it could barely fit into her hands. Trina stopped kissing him and pulled his penis out of his pants. She kissed the tip of it and Allen squirmed uncontrollably.

Trina grabbed him and put her whole mouth onto it. She massaged his penis with her mouth and when she was done, she hopped on it and rode him until he climaxed. She didn't bother putting a condom on because she was on birth control pills and Allen was a virgin who couldn't transmit any sexually transmitted diseases to her.

By the time Trina reached her senior year, she had been with over 60 men and most were virgins. There was something about taking their innocence and witnessing their transformation into confident young men that fueled her sense of accomplishment. Her goal was to reach 100 before graduation. Although it was becoming more challenging as she grew older—most of the virgins were freshmen and sophomores—she remained determined and continued to pursue her goal.

During Trina's last semester at the university, she got a part-time job at the campus bookstore to help cover her extra expenses. One night, as she was leaving work, she was surprised to run into Mack. She hadn't seen him in almost five years since their prom night when he took her virginity. He looked different. He'd lost some weight and did not dress as well as he did in high school. She greeted him curiously, and he asked if he could take her out for dinner when she got off of work. Trina hesitated. She mentioned how he had treated her on prom night. Persistent, Mack kissed her hand and said, "It's just dinner." Eventually, she agreed.

Trina met him at the Burger King across the street from campus. It was all Mac could afford. They reminisced about the good times they had shared in the past. Mack mentioned that he had a steady job as an auto mechanic but was feeling the need for a vacation. When he learned that Trina was in Atlanta, he decided to surprise her. He admitted that he missed her and apologized multiple times about how he'd treated him on prom night. Trina was happy Mack apologized and admitted she missed him too. Mack was her first boyfriend, her first love, and her first everything.

By midnight, Trina had finished her kids' meal and told Mack she would call him tomorrow. She needed to leave since she had work early in the morning. Mack asked her why she was rushing, suggesting she might be going to see another guy. Trina giggled and assured him that wasn't the case. She explained she had a final exam to prepare for and had to work in the morning. Mack hugged her tightly, kissed her on the forehead, and wished her goodnight. Trina then got into her Uber and headed back to her apartment.

An hour later, Trina received an Instagram message from Mack. The message read that his motel room was no longer available and that he had nowhere to go. Initially, she told him she couldn't help him, but Mack begged and pleaded with her. Trina heard the rain pouring in the background, and her feelings of sympathy began to grow. After some hesitation, she asked him for his address and arranged for an Uber to bring him to her place.

Mack arrived at her apartment 30 minutes later. When he stepped inside, Trina insisted he take a shower, as he smelled like he had been living in a garbage can.

After Mack showered, he joined Trina in bed, where she was busy studying. She told him he would be sleeping on the couch, but he noticed she seemed stressed about her final exams. He offered to give her a back massage. Before she could respond, he began rubbing her back. She wanted to tell him to stop, but it felt too good to resist. Trina removed her glasses and lay across the bed, allowing him to massage her entire back.

Before she realized it, Mack had taken off her shirt and was rubbing coconut oil over her skin, kissing her softly with each touch. Trina rolled onto her back, and they began to kiss. Just then, Mack's phone rang, but he quickly silenced it and continued kissing her, moving down from her neck to her chest while holding her close. Everything felt so right—he was more intimate and gentle this time, and he made Trina climax in ways she had never experienced before, awakening sensations she didn't know her body could feel.

Feeling overwhelmed with emotion, Trina wanted to repeat the experience again and again. As they lay together, Mack mentioned that he could find a job as a mechanic in Denton and they could live together. Trina thought it was a wonderful idea. Mack was also an excellent cook, which made her fall in love with his first love all over again.

The first few months were wonderful. Trina was done with classes and getting ready to graduate so she could head to Howard Law School. Mack had the house clean, smelling good, with dinner ready. It felt perfect—he was perfect. Trina wanted to ensure she was perfect for him too, so every night, she met his needs in the bedroom, and Mack loved it, often falling asleep right afterward.

After graduation, Trina landed a job at a law firm as a paralegal in Washington, D.C. Mack informed her that his mom was sick and he needed to fly back home. Trina offered to accompany him, but he declined, saying she needed to focus on work and school.

That night after Mack's plane landed, Trina didn't hear from him. She tried calling him the next morning, but his phone went straight to voicemail. She went to work as usual. She worked double shifts while she prepared for her move to D.C. When she got off, she still hadn't received any missed calls from Mack. Frustrated, she called him repeatedly, but there was no answer.

A few days passed, and Trina began to experience a burning sensation when she urinated. She couldn't stop scratching and, when she examined herself, she noticed some abnormal bumps around her vagina. She didn't have any health insurance. In desperation, she went to Walgreens and purchased some vaginal cream, but after a week of use, her symptoms only worsened.

Trina tried calling Mack again, but this time his phone was off. The operator informed her that the subscriber she called had been disconnected. Angry and panicking, she decided to go to the emergency room. After waiting for eight hours at the county hospital, a nurse finally attended to her. Trina was asked to provide a urine sample, and they took some blood for lab work. The nurse then sent Trina back to the waiting room, telling her it would be a few more hours before they had results.

To pass the time, Trina played on her phone, scrolling through Instagram posts until it died. Realizing it was morning and she had to be at work soon, she called in to inform her boss that she could not make it in that day.

After four long hours, the nurse called Trina back to a room. She changed out of her clothes and into a hospital gown, lying back until the doctor arrived. She explained her symptoms to him, and he informed her he would conduct an examination.

After a few minutes of discomfort, the doctor concluded that he would send her tests to the lab to check for HPV, STDs, and cancer. He suspected Trina had genital warts and mentioned she would need to have them frozen off. He also gave her an antibiotic shot. Disturbed by the news, Trina grabbed her phone and tried calling Mack again, but his phone was still disconnected.

Trina was upset with herself for allowing Mack back into her life. She berated herself, calling herself all sorts of names as she processed her emotions. A few hours later, the results from her recent exam came in. The doctor delivered the shocking news: Trina was HIV positive and had contracted chlamydia and herpes.

Trina had always envisioned a bright future as a family law attorney. But everything changed when she received a diagnosis that felt like a thunderclap.

Facing the reality of her diagnosis, Trina was overwhelmed with fear, shame, and uncertainty. She made the difficult decision to leave her dreams behind, withdrawing from law school and returning to her hometown.

Back home, Trina struggled with her health. The vibrant young woman who once thrived in the bustling University of North Texas, both physically and emotionally. Now, she felt isolated, her friends unable to understand the silent battle she was waging.

Trina often remembered Mack. She struggled with forgiving him for what he did to her. She thought of many ways how she could get Mack back for the pain he caused her. She even googled ways of how to avenge someone who broke your trust. But just as Trina sought comfort in getting Mack back, she received the news that shattered her already fragile world: Mack had passed away in his sleep.

The news shook Trina to her core, but the official story troubled her. Mack's family claimed it was due to a heart problem, but Trina knew the truth. He had been battling with his own health issues, silently fighting demons that he could never vocalize.

Heartbroken, Trina stopped taking her medication, resigning herself to a slow decline. Life lost its color and the vibrant dreams she once held in a distant memory. Every day felt like a battle she no longer wanted to fight. Trina understood she would never be the same. The story of her life was over.

Previous Books

Awkward Relationships Short Story Collection Vol. I
By: Valencia Lee

Magic in the Jungle
By: Valencia Lee

My Spiritual Awakening: The Truth No Longer Hurts
By: Valencia Lee

Closed Mouths Don't Get Fed: Selling Your Way Through Life
By: Valencia Lee